Border Love

Alice Wootson

Published by Prism Book Group

ISBN-10: 194009965X ISBN-13: 978-1-940099-65-1

Published in the United States of America

Contact info: contact@prismbookgroup.com

http://www.prismbookgroup.com

CHAPTER ONE

BROOKE HUDSON DREW her gun and crouched behind a thick bush, grateful for the tropical climate of Brownsville, Texas. She pressed her face so close to the ground, she could smell the musty odor of the rotting leaves that covered this section of land.

The footsteps that caused her to take cover came closer. Birds scattered from the ground into the air, announcing the path of the person approaching. The steps were slow, but the person didn't try to keep quiet. Brooke frowned.

Even illegal intruders who got lost knew to move quietly. She shifted softly until she faced the sound.

She thought of a week ago when an officer's body was found thirty miles north of her current location. *Lord, please be with me.* She pulled her mind back to the sounds, eased behind a vine-covered tree, and waited.

When the noise was almost on top of her, she stood with her back against a tree and aimed her weapon at the direction of the sound coming through the brush. She waited and watched. A final thrashing through a thick clump in front of her sent a ground squirrel scampering across the tiny clearing and brought the person almost out of cover.

"*Para!* Halt! *No te mueve!* Don't move!" Brooke ordered just as a young woman stepped into view. "Are you alone?" she asked in Spanish as she scanned the area surrounding the woman. Then Brooke looked back at her and frowned. This wasn't a woman. This girl wasn't even in her teens.

Brooke scanned the area again. Mexico was only a few hundred yards on the other side of the road, but nobody this young would cross alone. Somebody was with her. How many? And where were they?

She drew in a deep breath and released it. Then she went to the girl, secured her hands behind her back, then stepped away, again using the tree to protect her from the rear.

From that position, she threw questions at the girl in rapid succession, but slowed her interrogation when the girl's eyes filled with fear as she kept her gaze glued to Brooke's gun.

Brooke tried again. No matter how she worded the questions, the answers were the same. The girl was separated from her family when they heard someone approaching as soon as they crawled through the opening in the fence. Her mother and father told her to run across the road, and she did. Then she couldn't find them or her little sister and brother. The girl sobbed and Brooke controlled the twinge in her heart.

After having her prisoner sit on the ground, she stood with her back against a tree. No unusual sounds reached her. She waited a little longer. Satisfied they were alone, Brooke moved the girl to the road. Once there, she scanned the area again. Then she called for pick-up as per procedure. They were too far from her vehicle to chance moving through the brush with a prisoner, even a young prisoner. Growth could provide cover, not just for herself, but for others. The road could be even more dangerous.

She had the girl sit on a slight hill and tried to ignore her soft sobs as they waited. The surrounding quiet did nothing to hide the sound, but Brooke figured she would have heard it in the middle of Fourth of July fireworks. Why didn't the patrol car hurry? She wished the child were older and someone else had caught her. Only her imagination made the waiting time seem like hours.

When the patrol car arrived, the girl's crying grew louder. It only took a few minutes to place her in the back, but time seemed to crawl during the ride to Brook's car. She avoided looking at the girl. Why hadn't she parked a few feet away rather than several miles?

Brooke drove to headquarters, reported for debriefing, then filed her report. Through it all, the girl's image stayed with her.

Forty minutes after reaching headquarters, Brooke sat on a bench in the locker room. The agents coming on duty for the second shift had reported long ago. Those going off duty were gone too. Still she sat.

I've been doing this too long. Maybe I'm burned out. A pair of large brown eyes, haunted deep within, rushed back to her mind. She shook her head. *I've only been at this for six years, but today it seems like thirty.* She leaned forward, placed her elbows on her knees, then hung her head. Maybe even forty. The door opened behind her, but she didn't look up. *Lord, is this where I'm supposed to be?*

"Hey, girlfriend, you still here? What's up?" Leah Delaney sat on the bench beside Brooke and nudged her.

"Hi, Leah," Brooke glanced at her friend. "You're late." She tried to smile, but didn't quite manage.

"We got bogged down in the field. Do I need a note from home? Hey, what's the matter?"

"Ever have one of those days?"

3

"You mean like today, yesterday, last week's entire shift, the week before that..." She frowned. "Where you going with this?"

"Do you sometimes wonder if we're doing the right thing?"

"About what?"

"Sending people back."

"No. We have to. We have no idea why they're trying to get in. That's why we have procedures in place. Think of the many times the patrol caught drug smugglers."

"Yeah."

"And I know you remember the three terrorists they caught four months ago."

"None of that applies to today."

"What happened?"

"I caught a twelve year-old girl. At least she said she was twelve. She didn't even look that old. She got separated from the rest of her family." Brooke frowned. "I doubt if they were bringing in drugs." She sighed. "I was so tempted to let her go..." Brooke shook her head and sighed. "There was something in her eyes..." She shook her head again. "I never saw such sadness before."

"Go where? You were tempted to let her go where? She was alone. I know she didn't have a map because those 'coyotes' who arrange the crossing—and charge big bucks, I might add—only give one to a group if that, and her parents probably had it. And I don't have to tell you how inaccurate those things are, anyway."

"I know. I've seen quite a few of those so-called maps. Still..."

"Let's take this further. If she had a map and managed to reach somebody who wasn't an agent, what do you think would happen to her? You know what the chances are that she'd be forced into prostitution. We've heard the statistics." Leah frowned. "Coming in contact with one of those situations is unsettling." Her voice lowered. "And I've helped stop more than one prostitution ring."

"My head knows your right. My heart is another thing."

Leah stared at the gray lockers facing her. For a little while, the only sounds in the room were drifting from the hall as people passed by. Finally, she spoke again. "You know how, on airplanes, they go through the emergency procedures?"

"Yeah?"

"You know they tell passengers that, if they're traveling with kids, they should put their own masks on first. Right?"

"Yeah?"

"That's because if they don't take care of themselves first, they can't take care of anybody else."

"Where are you going with this?"

"If we don't take care of our citizens first, make sure they have jobs and the economy is good, how can we help other countries? Right?"

"I guess so. Yeah."

"You know so. I'll bet the girl didn't even have a water bottle. Right? I know she didn't have any food."

"Yeah."

"Brooke, you saved her life. She won't be another body someone finds north of here, or a kid messed up by pimps." Leah patted Brooke's shoulder. "You did the right thing." She stood. "Enough of this. We're the good guys. Remember that. Let's go get some dinner. I'm starving."

Fifteen minutes later, they were sitting in Ida's Soul Food Restaurant. By unspoken agreement, their conversation during the meal didn't touch on the shift they'd just finished working. That didn't stop Brooke's mind from drifting there, though. No matter how she tried, she couldn't erase the image of that young girl's eyes. She continued to force herself to eat.

"Wow. You must have been hungry," Leah said half an hour later.

"Huh?"

"You really worked up an appetite today, didn't you?" She pointed to Brooke's plate.

Brooke looked at the empty dish and frowned. Not a crumb was left, and she hadn't tasted any of it. She set her napkin beside her plate. "I guess so."

Leah shifted her slice of sweet potato pie in front of her. "The food was exceptionally good today, wasn't it?"

"I'm thinking about asking for a town patrol assignment," Brooke said. She looked at her pie, but didn't even pretend to eat.

"You think that would be better for you?"

"It couldn't be worse."

Leah smiled. "I hear it's kind of boring."

"After today, boring sounds kind of good."

"Why don't you wait a while?" Leah touched Brooke's hand. "Until what happened today isn't so fresh in your mind."

"Even if I request it, you know it'll be a while before something opens up. When it does, I'll still have the option of not taking it."

"True. Still, why not take a few days to think about it?"

Brooke looked at Leah. "I've had this in the back on my mind for a while. I think now's a good time to make a change. I have to pray on it. I really need the Lord's guidance on this."

"Let me know what you decide." She stood, but she looked at Brooke's pie. "I know you're gonna take that with you."

"Absolutely." Brooke asked for a take-out container.

"If you put in a transfer request, what shift will you ask for?"

"First." Brooke smiled. "You and I will still be able to get together."

"Good. We can keep each other caught up on our exciting personal lives."

Despite her somber mood, Brooke laughed. "I can do that right now." She paused dramatically. "Okay. That's it for mine. Now it's your turn." This time they both laughed. It felt good.

"Unfortunately, mine is the same as yours." Leah frowned. "I thought we would have found somebody by now. We should have checked statistics more thoroughly to find out where the single men are."

"They're probably some place where it's cold." She paused. "You know, maybe we aren't supposed to get married. As my Aunt Hilda said, 'Regardless of the old saying, there is *not* a lid for every pot.'"

"I refuse to accept that."

"It would be nice to have somebody, but I can be okay with my own company."

"I'm not giving up that easily."

"No sense discussing this. What the good Lord has in mind, will be." The waitress brought the container. Brooke slid her pie into the Styrofoam box and stood. "Let's go."

"Sure." Leah stood too.

As they walked to the car she asked, "You got exciting plans for the weekend?"

"Oh, yeah." Brooke nodded. "My laundry is waiting." They got in the car. "Oh. Let me continue to answer your question. Don't leave out the vacuum cleaner and broom and mop and dust cloth..."

"Enough." Leah started the engine. "That sounds too much like the kind of weekend facing me."

CHAPTER TWO

Two months later

As DARIEN MCKEE stood on the sidewalk outside Border Patrol Headquarters in Brownsville, he asked himself the question he'd recited more times during the past six weeks than he could remember. *Man, what got into you that day?* He shook his head. He always came back to the same answer.

He encountered one too many bodies in the Arizona desert. Or, as in the last case, a truckload of bodies, and he lost it, plain and simple.

Darien wiped his eyes as if he could erase what he saw when he opened the truck's door. The sight and the heat and the stench hit him as the vulgarity of it came to his mind now, as it did too often.

So many people were crammed into the semi they would've had to take turns sitting. Darien blinked. If his partner hadn't pulled him off that truck driver when they apprehended him a few miles away, Darien would have killed the man. He exhaled a sharp breath.

He *still* wasn't sure he *had* acted wrongly when he grabbed the driver. That was the bigger problem. He shook his head. The agency frowned on killing suspects, no matter what the situation. There was a reason why agents were encouraged to change assignments regularly. That incident drove the point home. Still frowning, he walked toward the building.

Maybe in this sector he'd encounter illegal immigrants who were a danger to national security. Maybe he wouldn't just capture ordinary people looking for a way out of the poverty south of the border. That's the kind of illegal immigrants he apprehended the entire time he was stationed in the Yuma sector. He hoped the ones he arrested here posed an obvious danger. How much longer could he continue helping to send people back to poverty worse than he could imagine? He wasn't sure he'd still have the chance, anyway. There was a good possibility he'd be a pencil pusher when he left this building. It depended on the commander. Darien didn't like his future being in someone else's hands.

He showed his ID to the guard at the gate at the bottom of the steps and again to the one at the building entrance.

Once inside, a clerk directed him to Commander Young's office. The guard on duty opened the door and announced him.

They procured an apartment for me, but I wonder if there are further ramifications for what I did. Darien walked into the office.

"Have a seat," Commander Glen Young said after the introductions. He didn't waste time. "What happened at your last duty station?" He touched the papers in the open folder on his desk, but stared at Darien. "I have your file, but I want to hear your slant on it."

Darien gave the facts of the last arrest he made. He didn't try to downplay his actions. He was wrong and he knew it.

After he finished, the commander stared at him a few seconds before he spoke.

"We have a different situation here. The patrols farther out apprehend illegal immigrants, also, but by the time they reach the town, they've already made connections of some kind. A lot of them have relatives here." He paused and stared at Darien. "You find yourself reaching the point you reached in Yuma, you tell your partner."

"Yes, sir." Darien felt a weight lift. He was getting another chance at regular duty.

Commander Young glanced away. "I completely understand your feelings, Officer McKee." His words were low. "I was close to that point myself more than once when I was out in the field." He looked back at Darien. "Remember this, all else aside—we can't get much information from a dead prisoner."

"Yes, sir."

"You settled in at your apartment okay?"

"Thank you, sir. I appreciate the effort."

"One of the perks that goes with the big bucks you make in the patrol." He smiled. "Take two hours to get settled in, then return here to meet your partner."

BROOKE STOPPED OUTSIDE the commander's office and took a deep breath. Her old partner transferred and she was getting a new one. That was fine with her. She'd still be in town, and having a partner who was newly assigned to the area affirmed the confidence Commander Young placed in her. She straightened her jacket and knocked on the door. She went in when invited.

Darien looked at the agent who entered and frowned. He expected a male partner. Not that it mattered. Business was business. If she got through the strenuous training, she was competent.

The commander introduced them. "Agent Hudson is familiar with the town. It's not big, and she's been patrolling here more than a month. She can fill you in on the idiosyncrasies. You two will work first shift until further notice."

Brooke offered her hand to Darien and he shook it.

"Welcome to Brownsville, Agent McKee," Director Young said. "I know you will be an asset for the patrol. You two are dismissed."

"Is this your first assignment?" Darien asked as they walked down the hall.

"No. I transferred to town duty six weeks ago. I considered resigning, but I was led to transfer instead."

"Led? By who?"

"God." She glanced at him, then away.

Darien waited for her to explain, but she didn't. He let it go. He had things he wanted to keep to himself too.

"Town patrol is a lot different from field work," Brooke said as she led him out of the compound. "We'll walk International Boulevard today." She stopped at the corner, and they waited for the light to change.

"Is there always this much traffic coming from Mexico?" Darien frowned as a steady stream of cars passed them.

"Day and night, but it goes both ways. It slacks off in the early morning hours, though it never slows to a trickle. Many of those coming in are workers on construction jobs in the area." She glanced at him. "Some are even students attending Texas Southernmost College or The University of Texas at Brownsville."

"I wonder how many of the workers decide not to go back."

11

"I wonder the same thing."

Finally there was a break in traffic. They crossed and walked toward town. The bench outside the bus station was full.

"So many bus passengers this time of day?"

These folks looked as if they had been shopping. Plastic bags were gathered around them as if it was the day before Christmas and they had crammed all their shopping into this one day. A closer look revealed food packages sticking from the tops of many. A lot of laughing, small children chased each other in the small space between the bench and the street.

"Mexico has restrictions as to what their citizens can take back," Brooke said, "but I've heard that many of their border guards look the other way." Brooke shrugged. "So many products aren't available over there. If they are, they're more expensive."

"This is a whole different world here than where I was last assigned." Darien shook his head.

"For me too, but it's just different kinds of problems."

They walked down East Monroe Street. Several nervous glances shot their way, but Brooke and Darien ignored them.

"If I didn't know better, I'd swear I'm in Mexico," Darien said because of the Spanish conversations flowing around them. "It feels as if we're walking down a street across the border."

"Years ago when Texas took this area, many people stayed. Some still keep in touch with relatives across the border, and they visit freely back and forth."

"I imagine many of those who come across don't find their way back."

"From time to time we do spot checks and catch somebody who proves that true."

They crossed Fourteenth Street. When they reached a storefront just on the other side, Brooke stopped. Piles of clothing were heaped in the window.

"Look inside."

Darien glanced at the handwritten signs posted on the windows. Then he moved closer. Large, roughly-built bins lined the walls. More formed aisles from the front to the back of the shop. Mostly women, but some men, picked through the piles of clothing inside them.

"What am I looking at?"

"One of the largest 'industries' in Brownsville. This is where used clothing from thrift shops in the northern states find a second, or should I say a third, life. Things not sold there are bundled into huge bales and sold by the pound. These stores in turn tack on a profit and also sell them by the pound." She nodded toward the door. "Let's go inside for a quick look."

"Good morning, Officer Hudson." The man greeted Brooke, but looked at Darien.

"Good morning, Joaquim. Meet my new partner, Officer McKee." She turned to Darien. "Mr. Perez has owned this shop for years."

"Why so formal?" Joaquim held out his hand to Darien. His smile widened. "My name is Joaquim. Welcome to the neighborhood, as they say." Then he turned to Brooke. "I got a new shipment in this morning. Some really nice jeans. Some gotta be your size."

"Maybe I'll stop by on my day off."

He looked at Darien and frowned. "I'm not sure we got anything in your size. You used to play football?"

"Not since college."

"Stop in sometime. You might get lucky."

"Yeah."

"We gotta move on," Brooke said. "I just wanted to introduce you."

"Don't wait too long to check out the jeans," Joaquim called as they left the store. "You know how fast they're grabbed up."

"Yeah," Brooke called back.

"You shop there?" Darien asked once they were back on the sidewalk.

"Absolutely. You'd be surprised at the designer jeans that make their way down here. Some still have store tags on them. He's right about not wasting time checking them out. They get snatched up quickly by venders from across the border."

"I thought they were only allowed to take new clothes from here into Mexico," Darien said as they came to another used clothing store. He looked at a third across the street.

"That's what their government says." She shrugged. "I guess they decide which laws to enforce."

"How many stores like this are there?" Darien asked as he stopped walking.

"A new one opened up two days ago. That makes six. They're concentrated along this street."

"Six?" He frowned. "It must be the main business here in the Brownsville area."

"That and illegal crossings," Brooke said. She thought of the girl she arrested. "Maybe tomorrow we'll ride outside town so you can get a feel for the surrounding area. Our assignment is here, but you need to see what's around us."

Two blocks later they turned west onto Washington Street. "There's an interesting museum on this street," Brooke explained as they walked.

14

They passed a supermarket. Many of the cars in the parking lot had Mexican tags. Darien glanced inside.

"This many shoppers on a late Tuesday morning?"

"A lot of Mexicans like U.S. foods."

"Looks like a lot of merchants would be in big trouble if our neighbor to the south decided to enforce their laws."

Brooke smiled. "This would be close to a ghost town."

She turned south, and they walked toward Thirteenth Street. When they reached a group of three houses, she stopped.

"This is the Brownsville Heritage Complex. You should visit on your day off. The Museum has an interesting permanent exhibit." She turned to face him. "You know how our government complains about how difficult it is to extradite people from Mexico?"

"Sure."

"What you might not know is that the policy goes back to slavery times. You see how close the border is. Back then people were allowed to cross freely in both directions. Slaves who could slipped across the border. Once there, Mexico declared them refugees, just as Canada did. The Mexican Government refused to send them back." She smiled. "That policy was in place until just recently."

"They were more enlightened than our government. I'll make it a point to visit soon."

Brooke glanced at her watch. "How about lunch? There's a little café not far from here near the edge of town. I'm assuming you like Mexican food."

"Couldn't survive down here if I didn't."

They walked over to Adams Street and down to Ninth. At several places they had to step into the street to move around the crowds on the sidewalk.

At one point Darien turned to Brooke. "Tell me this is the lunchtime crowd."

Brooke smiled. "A lot of it. The rest are mostly shoppers." She stopped at a small restaurant facing Washington Park. "I thought we could order our food and sit in the park to eat."

"Sounds like a plan."

Despite the crowds, they didn't have to wait long. They sat on a bench under a tree and began eating. After a while, Darien broke the silence.

"Either this is extra good, or I'm hungrier than I thought."

"I don't know about your level of hunger, but this is extra good. Marietta is third generation Texan, but she claims that her recipes have been handed down through the family for many decades."

"You don't mess with success." Darien looked at her. "What happened to your last partner?" He took another bite from his quesadilla.

"Mitch transferred to foot patrol outside town. He said town patrol was boring." Brooke hesitated. "I was out there. I prefer boring." She paused again. "It was my assignment before I transferred here." Then she shrugged. "My partner from there is still on patrol northwest of here, out where it's not built up."

"How come the change? Tell me if I'm out of line."

"I don't mind explaining. It's probably not what you think. Brian and I were partners. Nothing more. He has a great fiancée." She stared at her tortilla. "It was time for me to move on." She frowned. "I stopped one too many poor illegal immigrants. One of the last times it was a young girl who got separated from her family." She looked at him. "It was either switch duty assignments or quit. I prayed for guidance and here I am." She looked away. "You about ready to go?"

16

"Yeah." They walked to the street. "You pray often or just about important stuff?"

"I talk to the Lord regularly." She smiled. "We'll follow Elizabeth Street and cut down Palm. That will give you more of an idea about the lay of the land around the town perimeter. When we reach Ringgold, we'll head back. By the time we return to International Boulevard, it'll be time to clock out."

"Fine by me."

Darien thought about what Brooke said about God. He couldn't remember the last time he prayed. He'd seen so much bad in the world, he wasn't sure God was still interested.

"The town tapers off as you reach the limits in all directions." Brooke's words pulled Darien back.

They walked along the sidewalk easily. No crowds got in their way since the lunchtimers had evidently gone back to work and not many stores were located there.

As they walked back towards headquarters in the easy atmosphere, Darien was beginning to feel as if he could handle anything that came his way at this duty station. For the first time since he had relocated to Brownsville, he began to relax.

Maybe his biggest problem here would be fighting boredom, and that would be fine with him.

CHAPTER THREE

As Brooke stood at the corner with Darien waiting to cross the street, a voice caught her attention.

"Hello, Officer Hudson." The young man lifted his chin and glared against the sun. "I thought you was off on Tuesdays." He didn't smile, which was unusual.

"Paco? Is that you? I haven't seen you for a while. My schedule changed since we talked last." She smiled. "I almost didn't recognize you. You were so proud of that moustache and now you've shaved it off."

"I like this way better. It looks cleaner."

"It makes you look younger. Are you still going to night school?"

"Nah." He shook his head and looked away. "Not for a couple of months."

"Paco, I thought we agreed you would get your high school equivalency."

"I might go back." He shrugged. "Or maybe not. It don't matter no way. They only let the poor get so far in this country." He looked at her, then away. "Besides, I don't have time."

"You still work for Joaquim in his store. Right?"

"No. Not no more. I got more important things I gotta do now."

Concern filled her mind. Paco couldn't be involved in the drug trade. Not when he had so much promise. Not when it was so dangerous. He couldn't. "What things?"

"Just…just some things." He looked at her for a few seconds and tilted his head to the side. "Just some things," he repeated.

Brooke frowned. "You told me that Joaquim was like a big brother to you."

"Yeah, well, I already got lots of brothers." He glanced around, then settled his gaze on Darien. He stared. "You new around here?"

"This is my partner, Officer McKee," Brooke said. She turned to Darien. "I met Paco when I was first assigned to town duty." She turned back to the young man. "So you changed jobs already."

"Yeah. You know how it is." He nodded slightly and glanced at the patrol office across the street. "You checking in? So you still on first shift like before, huh?"

"Yes. Going off duty in a few minutes." She glanced at her watch. "We're a bit early, but we have things we can do until it's time to clock out. I'll probably see you around, Paco." She touched his arm. "You stay out of trouble, okay? And think hard about going back to school. You know you're limited without an education." Brooke turned to go.

"Wait a minute," Paco said. Brooke turned back. "If I need somebody to help me with my schoolwork, you know, my math and English and stuff, think you can find somebody to help me?"

"I'm pretty sure I can." She smiled. "Tell you what. If I can't find someone, I'll tutor you myself. Deal?" She held out her hand.

Paco hesitated, then he took it. "Okay. Sure. Deal." Brooke turned away, but again his voice stopped her. "I see you in a big hurry, but I got another question."

"Okay. What is it?"

"Uh, how can I get in touch with you if I need to? You know, about the tutoring and stuff if I change my mind about school?"

"Just leave a message at the desk inside headquarters telling me how I can reach you."

He hesitated before answering. "Okay. I'll do that. So, you going off-duty, huh? You leaving kind of early today, huh?"

"You got it." She stared at him. "I already said that. You gotta stay focused, my young friend." She patted his arm. "You're too young for memory lapses." She smiled. "I'm gonna be looking for that message from you, so make it soon. Don't disappoint—"

A tremendous blast shook the area, slamming Brooke to the ground. Before she could assess her injuries, a second explosion scattered debris into the air, then a plume of flames shot up.

Brooke tried to look around, but thick dust hanging in the air almost blinded her. She squinted her eyes shut against flying shrapnel. More fragments, some lightweight, but others large enough to make her wince, pelted her back.

Her own deep cough echoed that of other people spread on the ground.

It seemed to take forever for the rumbling to fade. Even after it did, things continued to drop on her and around her. Gradually the large pieces stopped falling but smaller bits continued to rain. Still flat on the ground, Brooke searched the area.

The traffic light hanging over the intersection broke free of the line holding it overhead. In a shower of sparks, it crashed toward the street and landed on an upside-down car. The broken power line hissed and spit as if clearing a path. It writhed for a few minutes, then it quit and lay limp.

Street signs were ripped from poles and hurled onto the grass in front of the money-exchange building across from the small strip park. A store sign dangled by one side from a post. Shattered window glass covered the ground. It looked as if a cannonball hit the building. Falling objects continued to drop into the intersection.

Brooke lowered her head and covered it with her hands. Finally, the pelting slowed, then stopped, but she didn't look up again. Not enough time had passed for the dust to settle. She coughed as dirt clouds continued to drift.

Brooke, still hacking, lifted her head again and shook it to stop the ringing in her ears.

A woman sat on the sidewalk in front of Brooke with her mouth open, but Brooke heard nothing. She rose up on all fours and slowly looked around. She grabbed a tissue from her pocket and held it over her mouth and nose.

Tears streamed from the face of another woman and mixed with blood dripping from her forehead. Brooke scanned the rest of the area. Similar sights greeted her wherever she looked.

She paused her gaze at each person who lay in the street near her. It was obvious that some were dead. Still, she struggled to her knees to check on them. She tried to stand, but wobbled. *Father, please help us.*

"Steady." Darien grabbed her to keep her from falling again. "You okay?" He kept his hand on her arm. "I said, 'are you okay?'" he mouthed. A thick layer of dust covered his face and uniform.

"What?" Brooke shouted.

"You're hurt," he mouthed and gently touched her head. "Are you injured anywhere else? You got hit hard."

Brooke frowned at the blood on his fingers when he pulled them away from her head. She put her hand to the spot. The sting when she touched it told her where the blood had come from, but there was no pain. It would set in later in the form of a terrible headache. She'd worry about it then.

She frowned and continued to stare at Darien. Why was he whispering? Did he expect her to panic? She'd been hurt worse when she was a little kid playing with friends.

Slowly, the ringing in her ears faded and noises came to her. At first, they sounded subdued, as if underwater. They gradually cleared, but remained faint. Finally, it sounded as if the whole world shouted with more sounds all mixed together than she could have imagined.

Car alarms shrilled. Somewhere sirens wailed. The bells in the church two blocks away clanged, but a musician did not create the chaotic tune.

"Brooke? You okay? You took a hit to the head." Darien's voice rose above the other sounds crashing around them.

Brooke nodded, but she was sorry she did. It felt as if her brain bounced against the inside of her skull.

"You might have a concussion." He led her to the curb. "Sit here until help comes."

Brooke looked at a man surrounded by broken bricks, chunks of concrete and beams of twisted metal. His head lay twisted at an unnatural angle and blood trickled from his forehead. She glanced at other people spread out like a game of Pick-Up Sticks. *Lord, please ease their pain and suffering.* She looked at Darien.

"You and I are the help until then." She frowned. "Are you hurt?"

"No." He shook his head. "I was on your other side and a little behind you. I think you took the brunt of the impact for me."

22

"Okay."

Brooke let her gaze move to another man lying in the street. Her attention caught on a bit of sign beside him. She frowned. Only part of a word remained and a layer of dust covered it, but her eyes widened as she recognized it. She gasped as her gaze flew to the headquarters building, or what was left of it.

The foundation, still intact to a few yards high, showed the size and configuration of the building that had once stood. Piles of rubble filled the space as if someone had declared it a new dumping ground. A triangle of one corner of the structure still held its place as if waiting for somebody to continue with construction. A desk and a chair, visible inside near that corner, looked as if somebody had thrown them in and let them stay where they landed. The door beside the desk hung open as if somebody was about to enter the office.

Brooke continued to stare at the ruins. *Dear Lord, so much destruction.*

She tried not to think about who'd been in the building when she and Darien had left. She wouldn't make a mental count of how many staff members and officers were routinely on duty at the station at this time. Had she been in the building just this morning? She closed her eyes and said a silent prayer. Then she let her gaze pan to the right of the remains and a little beyond.

The blast had demolished the guardhouse that only this morning had stood solidly beside the bridge. It wasn't needed now, anyway, since huge piles of building materials blocked entry from the bridge. The last cars to cross over from Mexico, smashed as efficiently as a junkyard machine could do, peeped from the debris. One car lay on its side across the lanes.

"Paco?" Quickly, Brooke glanced around for her friend. She ignored the throbbing in her head the movement set off. "Where is

Paco?" Someone was stretched out on the ground in front of her, but it wasn't him. The clothes didn't match. "He was right here." A minute ago? An hour ago? Longer? She looked behind her. A man lay face down, but the different colored shirt told her that he wasn't her young friend either. Near the sidewalk, several people stirred, but Paco wasn't one of them.

"Let's see if we can help anybody." Darien tightened his jaw as he touched her arm. "Or do you think you should wait?"

"I can help." This time she knew not to nod.

Brooke headed toward what was left of the building. Darien grabbed her arm and she winced. He loosened his hold.

"Brooke. We can't go in there."

"Somebody might still be..." She inhaled deeply. "Somebody might need help." She started forward. "There are always people alive in the ruins in situations like this. Air pockets always form."

"Brooke, no. We can't go in there. Wait for rescuers with proper equipment. They'll be here soon." Darien tightened his hold on her arm again. "You don't want to chance knocking stuff down on them. Let's check those around us first. They need our help, and we can get to them."

Brooke stared at the rubble and released a hard breath. Then she slowly took in the chaos around them. Darien was right. "Okay," she whispered.

As Darien crossed the street, Brooke glanced at the remains of the headquarters building again and hesitated. Then she began looking for people in the open who could use her help. Several were dead, but many others were injured.

She and Darien improvised. They used hems of clothing to staunch bleeding. Most wounds on those who were conscious were not serious. Other injuries required innovation to control bleeding.

24

After she calmed a woman, Brooke showed her how to apply pressure to her young daughter's shoulder wound. Then she moved to the next person.

The sound of a siren approached but didn't get louder. It continued to split the air from somewhere north, but it seemed stuck.

As Brooke bound the head wound of a young woman who lay on her back on the sidewalk, firefighters on foot made their way through the rubble toward the intersection. One noted Brooke's uniform.

"You okay?"

"Yes." She nodded. The firefighter's gaze went to her face.

"You have a head injury. If you were this close to the explosion, there's a good chance you have a concussion. Maybe you should sit and wait until an Emergency Medical Team comes."

"If I do that, it means I'm not giving treatment. It would also mean I'd be taking help somebody else needs more than I do." She met his stare. "I'm okay. Nobody ever died from a concussion if they were walking and talking."

The firefighter glanced at the people she'd already treated and nodded. "They'll be bringing in equipment and supplies as soon as they can." He glanced at the building and frowned. "We couldn't get the trucks through, so our people have to come on foot."

"How far away is affected?"

"The worst is right here." He glanced at what was left of the building. "Right at what used to be headquarters. That was probably ground zero."

He looked at her a few seconds longer, then went to take care of one of the other victims.

Brooke glanced at Darien, who was assisting people across the street. Then she continued working her way through the others injured on her side.

CHAPTER FOUR

FOR WHAT SEEMED like days, Brooke worked her way through the victims while Darien and the other rescuers did the same. She forgot her own wound as she took care of those worse off. As she moved, she sent up a prayer for each one. She hoped what she did was enough to help.

A few small fires burned amid piles of rubble on the street and the sidewalks. The first priority had been to move people away from danger. The fires didn't grow higher nor did they explode, so Brooke assumed someone turned the gas off at a main line somewhere.

Brooke spent only as much time as necessary to stabilize a person's injuries, then she moved to the next. Often a cough helped her decide where to find the next person who might benefit from her help.

Brooke was grateful for the part of her patrol training that included emergency situations, but she doubted they anticipated something as massive and as serious as this when designing the program.

More emergency teams came on foot carrying supplies and equipment. Brooke was thankful for the additional hands.

She reached the edge of the damage, straightened, and looked at the others who were part of this rescue operation.

Together they formed a large ring around the victims. They'd stabilized everyone they could. As if they had met and discussed the next step, they began moving victims from the street and placing them on the sidewalk and grass in groups according to the severity of their injuries.

Finally, the faint sound of heavy earth-moving machines reached them. The equipment was a long way off, but it was coming.

Occasional clouds of dust above the tops of buildings still standing let those attending the wounded know the machines were moving material from their path as they tried to reach the scene.

Brooke breathed a little easier, knowing it wouldn't be long before they cleared the street. Then they could transport the seriously injured to the hospital. She prayed the wounded could hang on until that happened. Were the medical facilities still intact? More than one explosion had sounded, so she knew headquarters wasn't the only building hit.

She glanced at Darien, who was working with his back to her. His first day on the job was anything but routine. She frowned.

Please, Lord, let what happened today be a one-time incident and not a preview of more to come.

As they waited for the vehicles to show, Brooke and the others continued to work. Civilians who were able, despite their own wounds, helped move others. Those who couldn't help, but were conscious, sat on chunks of rubble or patches of grass, often holding a hand to their own wounds. Through it all, the voices of the rescuers questioned the victims. Only an occasional moan rose above the other voices. Brooke didn't want to think about what that might mean.

They had waited for it, but it still seemed sudden when a bulldozer pushed aside a tall pile of smashed cinder blocks and other rubble blocking the far end of East Elizabeth Street.

An ambulance moved into position as the earth-moving machine ambled to a smaller heap in the street and began clearing it. More ambulances pulled into position side by side.

Other patrol officers appeared behind the vehicles. Some were not in uniform, but Brooke recognized many.

They worked side by side with the makeshift rescue crews.

Slowly, piece by piece, they removed more debris from the street. Often it took two or three to move a chunk, but they managed. Finally, the street was clear enough to transport the victims out by vehicle. With the Lord's help, order had been pulled from the chaos. The first ambulance moved closer to the victims.

Those needing stretchers were moved first. Walking wounded went next. Many of those were transported in cars.

Someone began methodically covering bodies with blue tarps. Brooke swallowed hard as she watched. *So many, Lord. So many.*

Civilians who hadn't been in the area and weren't affected drifted to the site. Without a word they began helping those who could walk make their way to vehicles.

Dusk came and portable generators provided light on the remains of the building. That was all that was left to be dealt with.

The police department brought two German shepherd search dogs and took them to the headquarters, which now lay in piles of rubble. The dogs, starting at opposite sides, began sniffing their way through. Their trainers followed close behind. Each animal walked a few steps, bent close to a spot and sniffed. Then they moved several more feet and repeated the process. A few times they pawed a pile, but moved on. The trainers followed closely, but let the dogs do what they were trained for.

Brooke watched as one dog stopped beside a heap. He yipped and looked at his trainer. "Over here," the man called to several officers nearby, but it wasn't necessary. They were already on their way. Piece by piece they began clearing the small pile.

Please, Brooke prayed. Please, Lord.

After what felt like eons, she watched three officers lift someone from the wreckage. One supported the victim's neck, one the torso, and the third the legs. Brooke released the breath she didn't realize she was holding when the person groaned and shifted his legs as they placed him on the waiting stretcher. Cheers went up from the people around them. Even the wounded joined in. Hope surged. If there was one, there had to be more, didn't there?

Immediately after that, the other dog indicated a spot. More officers cleared an opening. It took four of them to move a large beam blocking the way, but they managed in little time. Then two other rescuers threw smaller chunks aside. They didn't stop until a large opening appeared. An officer reached into the space. Someone started out as the officer held their hand. Brooke recognized her.

"Mattie," Brooke whispered the name of an officer she often saw in the locker room. She moved closer.

"I'm okay." Mattie wiped her face, then bent over and started coughing. "Ben," she managed. "Ben was with me. He should be close." She gasped for breath and coughed again. A paramedic placed an oxygen mask over her face. She inhaled deeply, then pulled the mask aside. "We were in a big air pocket. Others are there too." Her coughing spasms stopped her words, and she put the mask back in place and took several more deep breaths.

"We'll get them," one of her rescuers said. "Are you hurt?"

Mattie shook her head. "Nothing major. Only the grace of God saved me." She looked at the remains of the building and blinked hard. They all watched as rescuers helped another officer out of the wreckage from the same opening. He was walking too. "Saved *us*, I should say," she said in muffled tones through the mask.

"Let's get you to transportation."

"How bad is it?" Mattie looked around again.

"You're looking at the worst of it." The rescuer shook her head. "You were *in* the worse of it."

The yips of a dog interrupted the conversation. He stopped at a spot, bent over, and touched his nose to the ground. He stared from the spot, to the trainer, back to the spot and barked. Rescuers rushed to him and moved the debris aside. The other dog answered from the opposite side, then found his own spot and yelped to his trainer. Rescuers dug. The dogs each moved on a foot or so and barked again. Survivors were freed from the rubble. The dogs barked and danced in place for a few seconds, then moved on after the last person was removed.

They continued at a steady pace. Several times the barks changed to whines and they lay down beside a spot without making another sound. Bodies were pulled from those places. Then the dogs moved to the next pile. They worked as if in competition, trying to see which one could locate the most survivors. Or bodies.

The rescue personnel no longer needed Brook's help, but, despite her throbbing head, she felt compelled to stay until the dogs finished. She cheered along with the others when someone was pulled out. Some she recognized, others she didn't. She saw Ken and remembered that his wife just had a baby girl. Donna used to work the same shift when Brooke was assigned outside of town. Many lived in the same apartment complex as her. The secretary who always smiled when Brooke checked in was rescued. When the search was called off, twenty-five had been found alive in what had been the basement. Brooke felt despair as bodies were uncovered.

Finally, late into the night, the team cleared the ruins except for the basement. The remaining piles of rubbish scattered over the pit were too small to hide a person.

Brooke stared in disbelief as the rescuers pulled out the last bodies, covered them with tarps, and placed them on the flatbed truck that had been waiting for this solemn duty. How could this have happened? Who would do something like this?

Half a dozen people stood in the aftermath and watched as the truck crept away. Then they trudged off without saying a word. The normally loud and busy intersection drifted into an eerie quietness.

"Let's go home," Darien said in a low voice beside Brooke. "There's nothing left for us to do here." He touched her arm.

Brooke stared at the place where the team pulled the last body, then looked up at him.

"Brooke, it's time for us to leave. Okay?"

She stared at him a few seconds longer, then took a deep breath. "Okay," she whispered, but still didn't move.

"Where do you live?"

"Down there." She pointed to a street on the other side of the intersection. "My apartment is on Lamont Street. The red brick building across the foot bridge..." She stared at the spot and gasped. "There used to be a little foot bridge there. It was so small that it didn't have a name." She shook her head. "It's gone."

"We'll cut through the university campus and go in the back way over the little foot bridge there. It will be all right." He touched her shoulder. "My apartment is in the same complex. Come on."

She hesitated, then went with him. *I can't damage anything. Everything is already torn apart.*

32

As they walked through the campus, the early morning seemed peaceful until Brooke looked at the dormitory construction. The blast had ripped down one wall that had just gone up a day ago and shattered a few windows, but no more damage was visible.

Brooke and Darien didn't disturb the quiet as they walked through the darkness. Brooke was grateful for the full moon since no security light came from the buildings.

Several light poles were down and a few trees lay with one side of their roots sticking in the air, but the buildings, at least the outsides, were intact.

They reached the edge of the campus, turned the corner, and looked at the bridge located there. It appeared as strong as ever. They examined it, then crossed and walked to Lamont Street.

When they stepped off the bridge and turned the corner, she stared at the apartment complex. It looked as normal as it had when she'd had left for duty. That was only this morning, but it seemed years ago.

Brooke paused and stared at the units forming a rectangle around the parking lot. The street lights were dark, as if they knew what had happened a few blocks away and didn't want to call attention to these buildings. Otherwise, everything looked as it should.

How could this area seem so peaceful when a few blocks away it looked as if the world had ended in a crash?

CHAPTER FIVE

DARIEN PAUSED ON the sidewalk before they reached the complex. "At first glance, it looks exactly as it did when we left, doesn't it? It's dark, but I think it would probably seem just the same in the daylight. Unless you checked it carefully." Darien's quiet voice broke into Brooke's thoughts.

"Yes." She continued to stare at the complex. Darien was right. Signs of what happened a few blocks away were absent, but on closer examination, the complex wasn't normal at all. Changes were obvious.

Landscapers had been at work when Brooke left for duty. Now palm fronds were scattered thickly over the grass, the sidewalks, and the parking lot. One large branch from the Sabal Palm at the far end of the lot leaned against Brooke's car. A smaller one was on the hood. Stones and smaller pebbles were strewn about as if somebody had hurled them during a tantrum. Many were on the cars. Here also a heavy coat of dirt and dust covered everything.

Brooke glanced at the way they would have walked into the complex if the other footbridge had been intact. Large limbs, ripped from the trees on the side nearest to the blast, lay with their jagged edges pointing away from the direction of headquarters, or what used to be headquarters. Branches and more fronds blocked the street at that end of the lot, but it didn't matter.

Nobody could approach any farther than to the point where the sidewalk ended in jagged concrete and dirt where the bridge had collapsed into the wide pond below.

Brooke was tempted to walk to the edge, but thought better of it. She'd seen enough damage to last forever.

"Which building is yours?" Darien asked, drawing her attention from the missing bridge.

"Building A." She forced her gaze to him. "Yours?"

"Building E. My apartment is at this end on the second floor." His gaze was steady. "You ready to go inside?"

"Yeah." Brooke swallowed hard, then walked to the steps in the center of the building. She stood at the bottom for a few seconds, took a deep breath, and slowly climbed to the second floor.

When she reached her door, she pulled out her keys. Instead of opening it, she stood with them clutched in her hand.

"You think your Henry O. Tanner original got tossed from your wall?" Darien smiled and touched her arm. "Is that why you're not going inside?"

In spite of the situation, Brooke smiled. "How did you know he's one of my favorite artists? I do have a copy of his 'The Banjo Player' hanging in my living room." She frowned. "At least it was there when I left. Who knows if it's still there?"

"We will—as soon as we go inside."

"Yeah." Brooke took another deep breath, then unlocked the door.

The light coming in from the open door showed her little entry table lay on its side. The pine needle and sweet grass basket she kept for mail and her keys was against the opposite wall.

She put the table back in place and flicked the light switch, but nothing happened. The electricity was out. The flashlight from the drawer provided light.

The figurine of a young ballerina, usually beside the basket, lay in the middle of the floor, its raised arms broken off. Brooke picked up both pieces and held them close to her chest.

"My sister, Bobbi, back in Philadelphia, gave this to me as a housewarming gift." She placed the pieces back on the table. "It's only a thing. It was never alive," she whispered. "It's not important." Worse things had happened. She closed her eyes, but when an image of the disaster appeared, she opened them again.

"Yes, it is important. It was a gift from your sister and now it's broken," Darien said.

Brooke opened the hall closet, pulled two lantern-type flashlights from a shelf, turned on one, and stood it on the table. It made the room almost as bright as day. There was no other damage. Except for the lack of electricity, the complex must have been spared.

"Thank you, Lord," she whispered.

"Let's have a look at your head." Darien touched her arm.

"My head is okay." Brooke touched the sore spot on her forehead. "It's not bleeding any more."

"We still have to get it cleaned up." He grinned. "You know— nasty germs and all. Lead the way."

Brooke hesitated.

"Not cleaning your wound won't undo anything. It won't change anything for the better."

Brooke turned on the other beacon and led him to the bathroom. As if in a daze, she took the first aid kit from the shelf, handed it to him, and sat on the edge of the tub. She flinched when he touched the antiseptic to her wound, but she didn't make a sound. This was nothing compared to what others had suffered. She sat with her eyes closed and let him take care of her.

"Finished." Darien pressed the edge of the bandage into place. "Since you didn't have any cartoon characters I had to settle for a plain tan one." He smiled. "You know the cartoons help wounds heal better, don't you? If you don't believe me, just ask any kid old enough to ask for one." He looked down at her. "Go along with me on this, okay?"

"Oh. Okay." Brooke inhaled. Then she stood and put the kit away. "Let's go into the living room. I want to make sure everything is okay in there."

"Right behind you."

When they reached the living room, Darien pointed to the large print behind the sofa. "I see Henry O. Tanner is still in his place." Then he pointed to another painting on the side wall. "Tell me about that one."

"Bobbi found that painting in a local gallery back home a few years ago. She said a picture of an African marketplace will give us an incentive to visit there one day."

"Did it? I mean, did you go?"

"Not yet. We plan to soon." She plopped down onto the couch. "Bobbi is a teacher, and she's bugging me to go next summer." She shrugged. "I don't know. Maybe I will." She covered a yawn.

"I should go home." Darien stood. "It's been a long day and an even longer night, and we've been working non-stop since..." He hesitated. "We should get some sleep."

"You want some juice?" Brooke rose.

"What?"

"I have orange and pineapple. Not mixed, but you can mix your own."

"Juice sounds good. It's been a long time since I had pineapple juice."

"Come on out to the kitchen." She smiled. "Today's your lucky day." She gasped and stopped at the doorway. "I didn't mean... I meant..."

"It is our lucky day. We're still here. Let's go get my juice unless you changed your mind."

"No. Of course not."

"Where are your glasses?"

"You don't have to help."

"I want to earn my keep." He frowned. "I mean my juice."

"I knew what you meant." She smiled as she put the pitcher on the counter. "You like cookies?"

"Does a pig like slop?"

"What?" Brooke turned to face him.

"Something my granddaddy used to say." Darien grinned. "No, he didn't raise pigs, thank the Lord. Whenever we passed by a pig farm on our way to town, I held my nose." He laughed. "Sometimes I had to hold it for twenty minutes." He shook his head and continued. "No pigs, but Granddad and my grandma had a flock of chickens running around the yard." His grin widened and he nodded. "High-falutin' folks would call them 'free range.' My grandparents called it letting the chickens fend for themselves as much as possible."

"Where was this?"

"Fitzgerald, Georgia. I used to spend my summers there." He closed his eyes. "My grandparents grew the sweetest corn in the world." He opened his eyes and looked at her. "You ever spend time in the South? I mean besides Texas."

"Yeah. Delaware." She grinned as she took out a bag of chocolate chip cookies. "My grandparents lived near Dover."

"If restaurants in that area served hash browns instead of grits for breakfast, they can't claim to be part of the South."

"Then I guess Delaware doesn't qualify." She frowned. "It's morning. We should be eating breakfast, not cookies."

"I'm not that hungry."

"Me, neither." She shook her head as she sat opposite him. "What do you think happened?"

"A bomb."

"That's what I concluded. Why *our* headquarters? Nothing that important goes on there."

"It's a government building. Why not?"

"Yeah." She nodded. "Good question."

"Maybe a better question would be who's responsible? It's not always the obvious."

"Yeah. Terrorists come in many different flavors." She frowned. "We've found that out in the past few years. When will it end?" She went over to the radio on the counter. "I usually use electricity for this. I hope the batteries are still good." She turned it on. "Maybe we can find out something." They didn't have to wait long.

"We will continue to suspend our regular programming in order to bring you the latest news as soon as it's available," a local newscaster said. "Authorities continue to analyze what happened on Tuesday." The reporter sounded as if he had been on the air for a long while, maybe since the blast.

Brooke and Darien listened as he shared the known details. Some of it they already knew, but a few bits of information about areas where they hadn't been were new.

Large terrorist bombs hit several other Border Patrol buildings in the area. Smaller bombs went off at other facilities in surrounding vicinities. Why target those specifically? Was that it or just the first of other attacks? If more were to come, what would be next?

When the reporter began repeating the story for the third time, Brooke turned off the radio, but she and Darien sat at the table staring at it as if it were still on. The juice in front of them was growing warm, but Brooke's mind was on more important things.

CHAPTER SIX

AFTER SITTING IN front of the untouched juice for a long time, Brooke jumped up and grabbed the phone from the counter.

"I have to make a call. The news of the blast was broadcasted all over the country. Bobbi will be worried about me." She looked at the answering machine. "Maybe she tried to call me. Maybe she left a message. I don't know. I-I have to let her know I'm all right."

She started punching numbers. When she held the phone to her ear, she didn't hear Bobbi's voice. She didn't hear a dial tone. She pushed the buttons again and again, but nothing came through. Then she tried her cell phone. Nothing. The display showed it was charged, but it wasn't functioning. She wasn't surprised the land phone lines were down, but she expected the cell phone to work.

The damage must've been more extensive than she thought. She frowned at the phone still in her hands. What to do? This news was bigger than big. It would have been reported around the world by now. Bobbi would be so worried. *What else can I do? Lord, please.*

She hurried to her desk and booted up her laptop, hoping to get a message to Bobbie that way. The hum when it came on told her that the battery was charged. She relaxed a bit, but not for long. The computer couldn't make a wireless connection to the Internet. The message that she should try later popped up. She tried again and again. In the past, sometimes she could make a connection right after the 'try again' message. Not this time, though. Each time, the same message showed. Proof of how widespread the damage was. Just as she started to give the command once more, Darien touched her shoulder.

"Brooke, maybe you should give it a rest. Electricity is needed to connect to the Internet, remember? You can do that when the power comes on, okay?" When she continued to sit staring at the computer screen, he squeezed her shoulder. "Let's save the battery and try later, okay?"

Finally she tore her gaze from the screen and glanced up at him. "Okay." Her voice was soft as she shut down the computer.

Mid-morning found Brooke and Darien sitting in her living room. Full daylight allowed them to turn off the flashlights. An eerie silence filled the apartment without the usual hum of electricity doing its thing.

"How well do you know Paco?" Darien broke the silence. His voice was low.

"Paco?" Brooke frowned. "Well enough, I guess. Why?" She turned to face him.

"He worked hard to keep us—make that to keep *you*—from crossing the street and going into headquarters. Why?"

"Paco?" Brooke frowned. "You think Paco had something to do with this terrible thing?"

Darien shrugged. "I'm just saying...think about it. Paco was surprised that you weren't off duty. He didn't expect you to be anywhere near the building. Fact is, he spent a good fifteen minutes talking to us. Why? What did he say that was urgent enough to keep you from checking in? And why keep repeating things?"

"But he's just a kid."

"Younger people have been pulled in by others who do all kinds of terrible things. Poor, high school drop-out with little hope for a good life—Paco was ripe for recruitment by some organization who could use him, who could make him feel important. They know which buttons to push." He looked at her. "Brooke, I've seen it before. Those who know how to brainwash don't discriminate according to age or anything else. In fact, they go after the vulnerable."

"I know about their recruitment practices, but Paco?"

"Where did he go so fast? One minute he was there, then after the blast, he was gone." Darien shook his head. The crease between his eyes deepened. "Actually, he telegraphed what was going to happen. We just didn't get the message."

"How did he do that?"

"Think back. While he was talking to you, he kept glancing at the building. A couple of times he looked quickly at his watch." Darien urged her with his eyes. "Where did he go after the explosion? Did he take off as soon as the blast caught our attention? Or did he leave before? He wasn't in the wreckage. You and I personally checked the area around us. You know we didn't find him."

"I hate to think he was involved." Brooke blinked hard. "I-I thought I knew him."

"Maybe you did." He shrugged. "You hadn't seen him for a while. Who knows what he was doing during that time, or who he was talking with."

"I don't know. I never thought Paco..." She shook her head. "Not Paco."

"We don't know for sure," he said. He looked at his watch. "It's late. Or should I say, early. I should be going."

"Wait. Don't go." She wasn't ready to be alone. "I'll fix us something to eat. It's been a long time since we had lunch. What I prepare will be cold, of course, but I have the makings of salad and sandwiches." She stood.

"Sounds good." Darien followed her into the kitchen. "Need any help?"

"No, just sit."

She gathered what they needed for the meal. Then she sat opposite him.

Brooke bowed her head. "Lord, first we want to thank You for sparing us through the explosion. We thank You for the ones You saved and for using us to help. We ask for Your blessing and Your comfort for the families who lost loved ones." She paused. "Please guide our leaders as they move forward." She hesitated. "Lord, I ask You to take care of Paco." She paused again. "We ask Your blessing on the food we are about to receive in Your name, Father. Amen."

Darien's echoing 'amen' was low.

Brooke didn't taste any of her food, and she doubted if Darien did either, but she knew it was essential to eat if they wanted to keep functioning. They finished, then cleared the table.

"I know we're operating on fumes, having had no sleep since forever," Brooke said as she gave the counter a final swipe with the dishcloth, "but don't you think we should report in? I'm sure they told you about the contingency plans when you first reported for duty."

"Yes, but I haven't had a chance to locate where we go. Let's ride together."

"Okay. I'll drive us to the Harlingen office since I know where it's located. I took a run up there on my first day off. It's about ten miles up the road."

"Is your head okay?"

"It's barely letting me know that I didn't protect it." She smiled. "It's okay."

"Let me go take a quick shower. See you in a few?"

"Yeah. I'm going to do the same." She glanced at her watch. "Twenty minutes okay with you?"

"Fine. I'm sure the hot water is long gone." He grimaced. "Got anything with caffeine? We need something to get us there and back."

"I have some cola. Too bad we don't have a way to concentrate the caffeine."

"We'll do the best we can."

Half an hour later they were on the road. They attempted several streets, but had to back up when they couldn't get through. The blast had destroyed the fronts of buildings closest to the explosion, rendering them piles of rubble.

Merchandise from display windows lay in the street on top of bricks that'd been part of destroyed structures. A pink tricycle, flung from a toy store, lay on its side. It looked as if a child had fallen off and run home for some sympathy.

Finally, after trying numerous roads away from the center of town, Brooke was able to squeeze through four blocks from the blast site. She had to weave off and on the sidewalk part of the way.

As they passed small intersections, they caught a glimpse of the extended damage. It looked bad when she took a quick look, but Brooke knew it was even worse than it appeared at first glance. She tried not to think of the human toll that was far more important than the destruction of buildings and vehicles.

Debris littered the streets and sidewalks. Downed trees were everywhere, many on top of cars. Brooke hoped nobody had been in the ones with the caved-in tops.

Gradually they saw less damage, and they reached an area where trees still stood at the curbs as they were supposed to. Many had lost branches, but they were secure in the ground.

Brooke turned a corner and the way was clear. They took Route 77/83, heading for Harlingen and the Immigration and Customs Office located there.

A new checkpoint was located three miles from the office, another was in place two miles out, and a third a mile from the government complex. Concrete barriers were in place so no one could drive straight through. Instead, Brooke had to slow to a few miles an hour and weave her way through as if this was part of a driving test.

They were detained at each checkpoint and their identity checked from a list each guard carried. When they were finally allowed access to the parking lot, officers verified their identities again. A final check was made before they were allowed to enter the building. They joined the slow, silent stream of others.

Personnel sat at each desk and more were stationed at each door. A low mixture of sounds carried through the room as people checked in. The hum of machines, papers shifting and footsteps as people moved about added to the low noise.

A guard directed Brooke and Darien to the auditorium. The guard there checked their identities once more before they were allowed in.

The room was full. At least these people were all right. Brooke scanned those seated, looking for familiar faces. Her gaze stopped, and she exhaled when she saw Leah in the middle of a row. She hurried toward her.

Leah spotted her and rushed over They hugged each other in the aisle and rocked from side to side.

"I am so happy to see you." Leah's voice broke.

"Not any happier than I am to see you."

Finally they pulled apart. Brooke noticed tears in her friend's eyes. Moisture gathered in her own. She turned to Darien. "This is my new partner, Darien McKee."

The three made their way to the back of the room.

"Where were you when it happened?" Brooke asked as they sat.

"I was off duty, but I was going in to catch up on some paperwork..." Leah paused and took a deep breath. "At the last minute, I decided to go across the border to Matamoros and do some shopping instead." She paused again. "I just reached my car when an explosion rocked the area. It sounded as if it was at the International Bridge, but buildings were damaged. I walked back toward town." She glanced at Brooke. "You know how the marketplace is always crowded? Many people were injured by falling debris. Some were killed. I helped free people as much as I could. I went to the bridge, but the guardhouse was down and it and cars blocked the way. I worked my way along the border fence until I could find a shallow place to cross the Rio. I climbed the fence back over to our side." She shook her head. "From there, I caught a ride with an agent who was called back from patrol. Route 77 was blocked, so we continued on foot. When we reached Seventh Street, we stopped to help." She swallowed hard. "There was a lot of damage in that area and too many casualties for us to count." She glanced at the floor, then back up. "We just kept working, doing

47

what we could until help could reach us. How about you? Where were you?"

"Darien and I were going off duty. We were across the street from headquarters." She stopped and took several deep breaths. "After the blast there we helped those we could until medical personnel got through."

Ten minutes later, Commander Reynolds stood in front of the group. Brooke hoped the only reason he was in charge was because this was his post and not because something had happened to Commander Young.

"I'll get started." He paused. "Agents currently on duty will be briefed later. Briefings will be held as needed throughout the day." He scanned the group. "We're still examining the incidents, but preliminary findings point to a series of bombs. A large explosion took down the Brownsville Headquarters Building. Another damaged the International Bridge. A substation on Seventh was hit, also. Simultaneous attempts to blow-up headquarters in El Paso and McAllen failed. In McAllen the terrorists crashed a pick-up truck through the gate. An agent on duty took the vehicle out and it exploded before it was close enough to damage anything in our complex."

The auditorium could have been empty for all the sounds from those listening. It was as if a classroom of first-graders had been promised a big reward for being quiet and still. But this was nothing like a schoolroom, and any reward would be the apprehension of whoever was behind the terrorist attacks.

"The perpetrators got sloppy in El Paso and their bomb detonated while they were four blocks away from our complex," Officer Reynolds continued. "As is always the case in terrorists' attacks, many civilians were casualties there, also. No agents were hurt." His stare hardened. "Our office in Laredo wasn't as fortunate. It was hit. Hard. That bomb went off two minutes before the one in Brownsville. Commander Spanner had scheduled a special briefing for that morning, so more agents than usual were present." He stared at those assembled. "It's possible those responsible knew about the meeting. That's being investigated as we speak." He paused as if to give time for the information to sink in. "We lost a total of sixty-two agents yesterday. Many other agents are injured, some critically." He paused again. "We expect the number of fatalities to rise," he added. "The number of civilian casualties hasn't been determined yet, but we expect it to be high. Very high. Experience has shown us that these animals don't care who they kill." He panned the group. "My second-in-command, Officer Stafford, will continue with the briefing."

"You all know how thin we were spread before," Officer Stafford said without preliminaries. "This makes a bad situation worse. Members of the National Guard have been called up, but even if we pare their training down to a minimum, they will still need a lot of help from those of you already in the field. We've accelerated the training of the current class at the academy, but that too will take time."

He glanced at the papers on the table then back at those assembled. "Due to what turned out to be a fortunate traffic tie-up, or an act of God, our Brownsville office lost the fewest number of agents. Many agents on patrol in the field, as well as those on their way to report for duty, were delayed. The building is gone, but that can be replaced. Many of you within this sector will be reassigned. Those of you on foot patrol, especially in towns, will patrol the roads for now."

Brooke considered this news. After what happened, she knew she wouldn't have a problem going back into the field. The

49

bombings brought home the bigger picture of the importance of guarding the borders.

Commander Stafford continued. "Some of you will go on duty as soon as you leave here. I don't need to tell you to be extra alert. The entire world knows we're vulnerable right now. We don't know if this was it or only the first wave." His gaze hardened. "But we will find out. Any new assignment you receive today will be temporary. Other agents, mainly from the sectors along the Canadian Border, but some from others as well, will be reassigned here. They've had training, of course, but they'll need orientation to peculiarities of this region. Those of you assigned to Brownsville will report to an office we've set up in the National Guard Armory."

The new headquarters was as close to Brooke's apartment as the destroyed building, but Brooke felt no happiness over that. If it would mean erasing what had happened, she'd travel any number of miles each day to report for duty. She forced her attention back to Commander Stafford.

"Many personal vehicles were destroyed along with official vehicles. We'll manage. Outside help from other states is on the way, both official and civilian. Utilities will be fully restored and streets will be cleared ASAP. Even as we speak, convoys of vehicles are on the way from Houston and San Antonio. More will be arriving from further away. It'll take time, but we will handle things until we're as close to normal as we can get it." He looked at those assembled. "Questions?"

When there were none, he continued. "We have pulled your records from the computer files. When your name is called, you will report to the appropriate table among those set up around the perimeter of this room. May God continue to bless America."

Brooke sat in silence and waited with the others as the enormity of the situation continued to sink in.

We're in a war. An undeclared war where the enemy is not obvious, and all we can do is react to their actions.

As she waited, she again prayed for all those involved and again gave thanks for those spared. Things could have been so much worse.

CHAPTER SEVEN

AN HOUR AFTER they reported to headquarters in Harligen, Brooke and Darien's names were called.

"Stop by tomorrow," Leah told her as she left the row. "I don't know what shift I'll be on, but if I'm not on duty, I'll be home. Of course, you don't know which shift you'll be on either. Anyway, don't worry about how late it is. I want to talk with you." She blinked back tears. "I am so glad you are okay."

"I'm glad you are too. I'll call you," Brooke promised as she approached one of the tables with Darien.

"Have a seat." The officer said as he looked up from the papers in front of him. "I'm Jim Malone. I see you've just been assigned as partners." He glanced at each one. "You were on foot patrol in Brownsville, and Tuesday was your first day on the job together, Darien. Is that correct?"

"Yes, sir," they answered together.

He eyed Darien. "Your first day in this sector."

"Yes, sir," Darien answered.

"Heck of a welcoming."

"Yes, sir."

"We'll leave you with Agent Hudson until you're more familiar with this area." He glanced at Brooke. "I assume you're okay with that?"

"Yes, sir."

"You too, Agent McKee?"

"Yes, sir."

"Good." He nodded. "For the time being, we're pulling your team from foot patrol in town." He glanced at the map and the paper beside it. "Instead, you'll drive the area between Brownsville and Roma. Take the farm roads to 490, then work your way back to 77. Vary your route any way you think is best for effectiveness, just as you did on foot patrol. We have an added reason now—your safety." He paused. "Cover as much of the area as time permits." He pinned his gaze on Brooke. "That's the area you transferred from. Any problems with going back?"

"No, sir." She answered without any hesitation, her voice strong and steady. "I can handle it," she added.

He nodded. "Good. You two will report to the office in the National Guard Armory on Friday at 0700 hours. Because of your involvement in the aftermath in Brownsville, we're delaying your reporting for duty. Get some rest. You'll need to be in top form. We're extending shifts until further notice. Ten hours on and only one day off per week. The day off will vary. We expect to be able to make adjustments in approximately one month, when we get more people on board. Some agents will have to use their personal vehicle until we acquire new patrol cars. Every border vehicle in Brownsville not in use was destroyed along with any personal vehicle parked in the headquarters lot. Was either one of yours hit?"

"No, sir. Our buildings are walking distance from headquarters." She paused. "We're just as close to the armory." She took a deep breath. "Our cars sustained only minor body damage."

"Any problem with your housing?"

"No, sir."

"Good. Document your work mileage." He closed the folder on his desk. "Any questions?"

"No, sir," they answered together.

He handed them each a copy of their orders. "You're dismissed. Be careful out there," he added just before they turned away from the table.

As they walked away, Agent Malone called another name. Only one. Brooke tried to think of more than one reason why he hadn't called the agent's partner too. The best explanation would be the other agent was injured. She said yet another prayer and shoved the worst possibility from her mind as she walked into the hall.

They left the building and were in the car before either spoke.

"Our new area is where you were last assigned?"

"Yeah."

"What if you run into the same kind of problem that made you ask for a transfer?"

"I'll deal with it. I can handle it." Brooke's words were quiet, but strong. "After what happened, I can handle anything. Let's go home. My caffeine fix has worn off."

"I'm in the same boat."

They took the same route back to Brownsville. One of the streets they detoured around on their way to the briefing was clear enough to allow one lane of traffic through, but the others were still as they'd been after the bombings. It was going to take some time to get things back to normal, or as close to it as possible, because she didn't believe normal was possible anymore. Neither said anything during the ride home.

"Should I call you tomorrow so we can work out details for Friday morning?" Darien asked as they left Brooke's car in the apartment complex parking lot.

"Yeah. Maybe about ten. That should give me time to do a little catching up on some sleep."

"Me too. Talk to you then."

She went to her apartment and flipped the light switch, but she didn't expect anything to come on. It didn't.

There are worse things than not having electricity, she thought as she went into her bedroom. A lot more things.

She undressed and pulled on a nightshirt. After she said her prayers, she crawled into bed. She fell asleep almost as soon as she tugged the top sheet over her.

LIGHT COMING FROM the hallway nudged Brooke awake. She glanced at the clock on the dresser across the room. '12:00' blinked at her. She knew it wasn't noon. If so, she'd be at work. Midnight? Was it midnight? She picked up her watch and frowned as she tried to shake off the brain fog. 9:00. Why was it still dark at nine o'clock in the morning?

Then reality crashed in. It was nine at night, and she hadn't had a nightmare. The events that led up to her being in bed at this hour flooded her mind.

She sat, pulled her knees to her chest, and wrapped her arms around them.

It happened. The whole terrible set of events really happened. A bomb destroyed the tranquility of Brownsville and things would never be the same again. Lord help them all.

A few seconds later, she went through her normal morning ritual even though it was night. Her mind was so filled with the enormity of what'd taken place that it didn't register that she had hot water for her shower until she dressed. The electricity was back on. *Thank You, Lord*.

Minutes later she stood in front of the sofa, coffee cup in hand, staring at the television even though it wasn't on. Did she really want to watch the news?

She took a deep breath, sat down, and pressed the power button on the remote control.

A newscaster, who looked as if he had been up for days, sat behind his desk. Papers were strewn all over it rather than in the orderly pile usually visible to the viewing audience.

"We have footage shot by a team of local college students working on a class project." He gave the students' names. "As we show it, I'll describe it as best I can."

A picture of the headquarters as it was two days ago emerged on the screen. It was a long shot from the side of the intersection closest to town. Brooke turned at that intersection every day on her way to and from work.

A voiceover from a young somebody off-camera explained that the project was about modern day immigration from Mexico to this area of Texas.

"This is the current Border Patrol Headquarters building located beside the International Bridge that allows access to and from Mexico. Foot traffic as well as..." A loud explosion sounded. The camera wobbled and must have fallen to the ground because it showed a sideways view of the building. The shot was close to the ground, but it was obvious to the viewer that an explosion took place.

Particles, large and small, pinged off the lens and scattered in front of it, almost covering it completely. Sounds accompanied the sideways picture, but were scrambled together, and it was impossible to sort them out.

As the scene of the chaos continued, someone must have set the camera upright because, even though the sounds of shouting, cries, things crashing, and others noises blended together, the picture was straight again.

Brooke clinched her hands as the scene she and Darien had so recently lived through appeared on the screen. The picture continued to wobble, but the destruction was captured perfectly.

Heaps of concrete slabs, rocks, huge pieces of metal, dirt, shards of glass, signs, every kind of material that goes into building a manmade structure, was present in some form. The scene looked like the beginning of a wide landfill.

As Brooke watched, she thought of those who had been pulled out of the wreckage alive. *How did anybody at all survive what I'm looking at? Why wasn't everybody killed? I was right there. How was I able to walk away?* Those questions raced through her mind as she stared at the scene of destruction. Only God. The newscaster's voice sounded again.

"We thank the students for making this film available to us." The reporter said off-camera. He paused. "Two of the four-member team of students are in the hospital." He paused again. "This next footage was filmed by our own crew when they reached the scene after the video you just witnessed." He glanced at the papers on his desk, then back to the camera. "We have neither names nor a count pertaining to casualties as yet, but we do know they could've been higher. A four-vehicle traffic accident a block away from Patrol Headquarters prevented many agents who were on the first shift from reporting in and the second shift had already left for duty."

His voice lowered. "The toll could have been worse," he repeated. "Much worse if not for that accident."

But for God... Brooke sent up a silent prayer of thanks.

"We'll..." The reporter stopped talking and took several deep breaths. "We'll keep you posted, as soon as we have more information." He gave his name and station identification. Then a commercial appeared on the screen.

The phone rang and Brooke was glad for the interruption, which also indicated the phone was on again.

"I took a chance that you were awake," Darien said.

"I woke up a little while ago." She hesitated. She didn't want to be alone right now. "Want to come over?"

"Yeah. See you in a few."

She hung up, called her sister, and spent ten minutes trying to convince a hysterical Bobbi that, yes, she was all right, and there was no need for either one to travel to prove it. As she broke the connection, the doorbell rang.

Five minutes later, she and Darien were sitting in the living room, coffee cups in their hands.

"Did you get any sleep?" he asked.

"Out like a light until the hall light came on. You?"

"The same. The body has a way of taking the sleep it requires."

"You got that right. Since power is back on, why don't I fix us something to eat?"

"Sounds like a plan," Darien said as he followed her into the kitchen.

"Omelets okay?"

"Great. What can I do to help?"

"Just sit. I'll have it ready in a few minutes."

"I'm not a 'just sit' kind of guy. I can at least set the table. Point me to the right drawer and cabinets."

"Okay."

Brooke told him where to find the things. It felt normal to prepare a meal after all that'd happened, even though it wasn't usual for her to cook for a guy.

"I know you just got to Brownsville," Brooke said after they were seated at the table and she'd said grace. "But have you had a chance to see the area outside town?"

"You mean the area we'll be patrolling?"

"Yes."

"No." He shook his head. "I've circled the perimeter close in, but I haven't been farther out. Except for where you took me on our first day, I hadn't seen anything of the town, either, except for what I passed on the way to and from the supermarket. When I moved here from the Yuma Sector, I took the highway, so I didn't see much of the area then, either." He ate a bite of egg. "Tell me about where we've been assigned."

"Our problems here are probably different from the Yuma Sector. Here, illegal immigrants might cross the fence anywhere along the border." She shook her head. "It's all vulnerable. The fence pretty much follows the river contour, so it twists and turns along the water's path. I understand it has always been difficult to patrol, but the river level has been so low for years that it's no problem to wade across at any place for miles." She glanced at her half-empty plate, sighed, and forked another bite. "I would say we don't have enough manpower, but the reality is, I doubt if there *is* enough manpower to be completely successful in stopping anybody determined to enter. All we can do is catch as many as we can."

"Many dangerous illegal immigrants caught?"

"Some, but not a lot." She took a deep breath. "Most are just ordinary folks looking to escape poverty in their country." Brooke sipped her coffee. "Tell me about your last assignment. Why did you transfer?"

"I almost killed a guy we apprehended."

"Okay." Brooke saw his struggle to keep his breathing even. She waited for him to continue.

"We found a small truck broken down in the desert. It was packed with illegal immigrants. I mean *packed*." Darien took in a deep breath. "It was too late for those inside. All thirty were dead from the heat. The guy didn't even unlock the back." Darien hesitated. "We followed tire tracks leading away. Two hours later, we caught the men who abandoned the truck." Again, Darien paused. "If my partner hadn't pulled me away from the driver, I would have killed the animal." He shook his head and looked at her. "If I had the chance right now, I'd try again. This time, I'd succeed."

"I understand."

"My commander suggested I transfer." He shrugged. "It was a strong suggestion, just short of an order. Since I'm not ready to change careers, I took him up on it. Maybe I'll work out here." He leaned back in his chair. "Aside from the lay of the land, tell me about the area we'll patrol."

Brooke described the ranches and farms positioned against the road on the U.S side. She told about the little towns and small shops that filled the needs of the people in that area.

"The business owners don't have to worry about a superstore putting them out of business. A chain store located there wouldn't turn a profit in such sparsely populated areas."

After they finished talking and eating, they cleaned up the kitchen together.

"Have you watched the news since you woke up?" Brooke asked as she hung up the dish cloth.

"For about ten minutes."

"Let's see it they have anything new to report. I want to know how this happened, what caused it."

"You and everybody else in the country."

They went into the living room, and Brooke turned on the television, hoping to hear an explanation for what turned their world upside down, but the newscasters kept repeating previous reports. Brooke was glad she didn't have to watch another showing of the students' film. No new information was available.

Brooke turned the set off. She didn't want to watch the pictures of the destruction over and over. She couldn't deal with images of what she'd lived through. She didn't need outside visuals. The whole scenario was stored in her mind, and she knew it would come back whenever it pleased. She prayed for strength to face it.

Darien returned home and Brooke went back to sit in the living room alone. It was quiet, but her thoughts were loud enough to make up for the lack of any sound.

Lord, what now? Please wrap Your protection around us.

CHAPTER EIGHT

BROOKE HAD NO idea how long she sat, but it didn't matter. The phone rang, and she was glad for the interruption of her thoughts.

"Hey, girlfriend." Brooke smiled at the familiar voice. "I didn't wake you, did I?"

"Hi, Leah. No, I'm just sitting here. I didn't wake up until after nine this evening so I didn't bother with trying to get back to sleep. After being up for two days my sleep pattern is all messed-up. I'm sorry I forgot to call you."

"My sleep routine is messed up too, so I forgive you." Leah paused. "These past few days have been unreal. Or at least I wish they were." A heavy sigh reached Brooke. Then Leah continued. "I'm glad you're still up 'cause I'm on my way over there as soon as I hang up. I'm dog-tired. I just got off duty, but I don't want to be by myself right now. See you in a few. Put on a pot of decaf. Better still, mix up a pitcher of something sweet, but without sugar, calories, and caffeine."

"Will do. See you in a few."

Fifteen minutes later, Leah arrived. As soon as she opened the door, Brooke pulled her into a hug.

"I'm so thankful that you're all right," Brooke said through tears.

"I'm glad you're okay too." Leah's voice broke and tears ran down her face.

Brooke pulled away a few minutes later and grabbed Leah's hand. "Well, come on inside. Don't let the flies in." She smiled and wiped her face.

A little later they sat on the couch, feet propped up on the coffee table, each with a glass of sugar-free lemonade.

"You told me you were across the street when the bomb went off."

"Yeah." Brooke hesitated. "Darien and I were getting ready to clock out. We should have been in the locker rooms or at least in the building at the time." She paused and stared into her glass for a long time, but Leah didn't rush her. Brooke spoke again. "Remember me telling you about Paco?"

"The kid with the crush on you?"

"We had that conversation many times. I still think he looks on me as a big sister."

"If you say so." Leah grinned. "Let me tell you about an object of my 'sisterly' feelings going back to when I was a sophomore in high school. Girl, there was this guy, Chandler. He was at the top of the senior class and the top of my super-fine list. He was also my neighbor. Unfortunately for me, he thought of me as a little sister." Leah sighed. "But I digress. I'll tell you the whole painful story someday." She sighed again. "Get back to Paco. What does he have to do with anything?"

"He was right across the street from headquarters. I didn't see him until he came up to us as we were waiting at the light to cross the street. He started a conversation."

"What's unusual about that? He knew you, and there is that 'crush' thing."

Brooke explained what had happened. Then she mentioned Darien's suspicion.

"He kept you from going into the building." Leah frowned. "Maybe Darien is right. It's hard to tell about people with things as they are nowadays."

"I don't want to think that about Paco. He's a likeable kid. I find it hard to believe he meant any harm to anybody."

"Sometimes we have to accept things we don't want to, no matter how strongly we wish they weren't so."

The room was quiet for a few minutes. Brooke's mind lingered on what happened and how she wished it hadn't.

"That's true." Brooke broke into the silence. "After things stopped falling, Darien and I helped with the victims." She stopped talking and struggled to find words that would hurt the least. "We were there when they pulled the survivors from the headquarters ruins." She didn't mention watching the dead carried out too. "How about you?"

"I told you I was in Mexico. After I did what I could to help over there, I climbed the fence and came back to this side." She paused. Brooke could tell Leah struggled to continue. She understood the feeling since she had just been there herself. She waited.

Leah went on. "The agent I caught a ride with was headed here. We didn't know what happened. As we got closer, the area looked like a disaster scene." She leaned closer. "Those words are too neat to really describe what we saw. It looked as I imagine an earthquake aftermath would. We tried several streets, but couldn't get through. We got a call telling us to report to Harlingen instead. Now we know why." She drew a deep breath. "When we got to Harlingen, radios in the shops were blaring the news." Leah's chin trembled. She went on. "We had to work our way around and through rubble. When we got closer to where the terrorists crashed, we had to leave the car and go on foot." She swallowed hard. "The injured in the street. The bodies. I..." She stopped talking again.

Brooke reached over and touched Leah's hand. Leah grabbed it and held it in a tight grip as if that was all keeping her from falling apart.

Leah loosened her grip then continued. "A lot of emergency vehicles were on the scene, but of course, this was more than they'd ever had to handle before, and there weren't nearly enough to take care of the injured. We stayed and helped as much as possible." She stared at the wall. "I don't know how long we were there. We did all we could until the emergency teams could take care of the rest, then we continued to the complex." She glanced at Brooke.

"You and I were doing the same thing only in different locations," Brooke said.

"After we reported in," Leah continued, "we were given details about the other bombs. When they said our building in Brownsville had been leveled, I was so afraid for you." She looked at Brooke and squeezed her hand. "I don't remember ever being so scared. I knew your day off had been changed, and you were working the first shift. I was so afraid you were caught in it." She wiped her eyes. "I knew you were signing off-duty at the time of the blast."

"I would have been. I *should* have been. Except for the good Lord. Maybe He worked through Paco." Brooke frowned. "Anyway, we did what we could for the victims. There were a lot of them."

"Yeah." Leah nodded. "Same with the area where we were. After we weren't needed anymore, we left and helped clear the streets as we worked our way to the Harlingen Complex. As they said at the briefing, no agents were hurt there, but a lot of civilians in McAllen were. You know how crowded those streets are."

"Always."

"But I don't want to talk about that right now," Leah said. "I don't want to talk about it anymore."

"I'm with you on that."

"Of course my partner and I got a new assignment, and they switched our shift. Today they asked us to work a weird one—noon to ten. Tomorrow we're working 11 to 8 and that will be our shift until further notice. When the agents report from the New Orleans Sector, we'll be assigned new partners until they become familiar with this area and our procedures." She shrugged. "Fred and I might never be assigned together again. How about you?"

"They changed our area, so I'll be back in the field, but since Darien just got here, they left us together for the time being."

"Well, I can think of worse scenarios than being partnered with him." Leah grinned. "He's a perfect example of a fine specimen of 'hunkdom.'" Her grin widened. "Or whatever the latest expression is. Any way you say it, he is enough to make the thoughts of a less professional woman turn to other than work."

"Leah." Brooke sighed, but smiled.

"Come on. You can't tell me that you didn't notice."

"I didn't notice."

Leah reached over and took Brooke's hand. She pressed her fingers over the inside of Brooke's wrist and stared at her own watch.

"Girl, what are you doing?" Brooke snatched her hand away.

"Taking your pulse to make sure you're still among the living."

"I had other things on my mind when I met him."

"One look at him should have kicked those other things way to the back. And that voice." She shook her head. "Mercy me." She released a slow, exaggerated breath. "That man's deep baritone gives a woman ideas that don't have anything to do with patrolling the US-Mexican Border. I hope the future has somebody like that waiting for you."

"He's all right."

"I'd take your pulse again, but I don't expect the results have changed. Maybe we should find a place where you can get your head examined."

"Thanks, friend."

"Just telling it like it is." Leah laughed. "When do you have to report for duty?"

"Friday morning."

"Good. Pop some popcorn, and let's watch that ancient Abbot and Costello movie you have on DVD." Her laugh had disappeared. "I need something light and silly about now."

"Don't you have to work tomorrow?"

"I have time to watch something and still get enough sleep. Remember, I don't report until eleven."

Two hours later, Brooke locked the door behind Leah. Half an hour after that she crawled into bed.

For the first time since I can remember, I'm not looking forward to my day off. I wonder if the crazies will try something tomorrow…maybe another bomb in a building. Perhaps someplace else around here that would have a huge impact. Or they'll try to hit some other part of the country.

She took a deep breath and closed her eyes. *Please let me remember: nothing's going to happen, Lord, that I can't handle with Your help.*

CHAPTER NINE

LATE THURSDAY MORNING, Brooke worked on laundry. Even in the aftermath of a disaster, routine chores needed to be completed. She just finished putting a load into the dryer when the phone rang. It couldn't be Leah. She was on duty.

"I didn't wake you, did I?" There was a pause. "Brooke? Are you there?" Darien added when she didn't answer. "Did I wake you?"

"Oh. Yes. I'm here."

Leah was right. He does have a deep voice. Brooke frowned. *Why didn't I notice that before? I still had the incident with that girl on my mind, then the bombing happened, but, wow... I should have noticed.*

"I did? I'm sorry. I guess, even if I hang up now, it wouldn't make a difference—you probably couldn't go back to sleep, huh?"

"No."

"I didn't think so. I'm sorry."

"No. I mean, no, you didn't wake me up. I'm doing my laundry. It's okay." *Pull yourself together, girl.* She sat at the kitchen table.

"Want to work out the details for tomorrow, or do you want to wait until later?"

Tomorrow. Tomorrow. Details for tomorrow. "Oh." Her frown disappeared. "You mean for going on duty."

"Yeah." He sounded confused, just the way Brooke felt. "Hey, look. If this is a bad time, you can call me. I'll be home most of the day. I have to catch up on some things too. I never finished unpacking."

"No, now is good for me if it is for you." She took a deep breath and hoped her train of thought stayed its course. "I'll drive tomorrow. It's easier for me to show you the route than to give you directions. After you think you've got it, maybe next week sometime, we can alternate. Okay?"

"Sounds like a plan. What time should I walk over tomorrow?"

They worked out the details, then Brooke hung up. Instead of continuing with her chores, she sat at the table as if waiting for someone to bring her a meal. Her thoughts weren't on food, though.

I'll have to see if Leah is right about Darien's looks too. Brooke rose to put another load in the washer. Leah was right-on about his voice. She sighed. *I hope he's not as fine as she thinks.* Attraction to the opposite sex is normal, but it was vital to focus on the job while on patrol. She frowned as she thought of what'd just happened. *I need to concentrate more than usual. I don't need to ride with a distraction.* She stood. *Maybe he's as ugly as a mud fence,* she thought as she went to fold her clothes. A face-only-a-mother-could-love ugly and with a terrible personality to match. She frowned. Looks weren't everything.

69

She didn't really wish that on Darien, but she wouldn't have minded if it were true. That way there would be no potential issue. Then she reminded herself, as an old song said, that everyone is beautiful in their own way. She smiled. Besides, God was *still* in control and *He* decided what would be.

She set about folding her clothes.

LEAH WAS RIGHT, Brooke thought as she looked at Darien looming in her doorway the next morning. *So what? This is work. We have to keep our minds on the job. Anything less than concentration could get you killed.*

"Am I too early?" Darien asked as Brooke stood in the doorway staring. "Should I have called first?"

"No, uh-uh. Not necessary. You're right on time. I'm ready." She grabbed her keys from the table, led him to her car, and drove to headquarters.

They checked in, then went to their assigned area.

Once on the road, Brooke forced her mind to stay on the job she was getting paid to do rather than on the man sitting beside her.

As she drove, she shared details about the areas they passed through, about the farms on the right, and the Mexico side opposite the twelve foot high chain-link fence on the left. She commented on how only a fence separated a country of wealth from a country of poverty. Then she left that subject alone as she followed the twisting of the narrow road as it mimicked the curves of the now shallow, narrow Rio Grande.

"I didn't realize how difficult it is to patrol the border here," Darien said after a while. He frowned as he looked at the river. "The Rio is no wider than a small creek and the cyclone fence has built-in toeholds." He glanced at her. "It doesn't help that there's no fence on the Mexican side, does it?"

"Why should they put one up? Only people at their bottom economic level and the undesirables want to leave. Our country has never prevented those types from leaving here, either. In fact, I've heard of municipalities in this country paying for transportation for people on welfare to move to other towns."

"Yeah. Nobody wants the poor, unless they can use them and exploit them."

Brooke drove a little further, slowed, then pulled onto the narrow grassy strip beside the road.

"Let me show you something." She walked over to the fence, and Darien followed. "Look." Darien watched as she tugged on a fence post. With little effort chain links, barbed wire, and all came from the ground. She folded the fence to the side.

"Looks like somebody made a gate without using hinges," Darien said as he stared at it.

"Unfortunately this happens too often, and it's almost impossible to detect as you drive past. A farmer put us on to this practice." She called headquarters on her cell phone. "They'll notify the local citizen's patrol. Many times they do the repairing. It gets done quicker if they do." She looked at Darien. "The owners have a lot of interest in keeping the fence intact, since it's usually their lands that get the foot visitors first. Their fields are destroyed, ripening crops are raided, and items from their storage sheds are stolen. The association will send out a repair team as soon as they can, but those coming over will just move their operation to another spot." She stared at the fence in both directions. Every inch was a potential entry spot.

"Sounds like a serious game of cat and mouse."

"Yeah. Too often the mice win, and we're not sure what danger they pose. For years there's been talk of electrifying the fence. Talk is starting again." She frowned. "I'm not sure it would be feasible,

71

anyway. I do know it would cost an enormous amount of money just to do the most vulnerable sections," she said as they walked back to the car. "After the hit we just took, I doubt that upgrading a fence is a priority, now."

"The ironic thing is, there's a good possibility that people who have been here for a while are responsible for the bombs and not newcomers."

"Yeah. History has shown there's no shortage of homegrown terrorists."

Brooke started the car and looked both ways, even though very little traffic traveled this road. It was used mainly by farmers with places next to the road and by illegal immigrants coming across the border.

"No matter which sector they enter through, most of those who manage to get here without being caught head north and east where there's less chance of them being apprehended and sent back. They provide cheap labor for businesses whose only concern is their bottom line." Darien looked carefully at the fence as they drove along below the speed limit.

"The property owners have a more immediate economic problem," Brooke added. "Illegal immigrants destroy and steal their property, and they have to dig into their pockets. It costs them thousands of dollars each year." She pointed to the section of fence they were passing. "See that? Some of the farmers have added ladders at intervals so the unwanted visitors will climb over rather than cut the fences. They pitch into the citizen's patrol, so it's money out of their pocket when they do."

"Does it work?"

"No way of really knowing. Some say illegal immigrants are suspicious and avoid them. It might be that..." The cell phone rang, and she answered through the headset. After a short conversation, she glanced at Darien. "We have to go to the Mendoza Ranch." She turned right at the next corner and continued down a narrower road.

"What's up?"

"Mr. Mendoza captured two illegal immigrants." She drove to an entrance about a half mile down the private road. An ornate 'M' decorated the heavy wrought-iron gate blocking the entry. An armed man standing beside it opened the gate and waved them through.

Texas Sabal palms formed a canopy over the wide road winding its way through the property. It took five minutes to reach the house.

Brooke stopped in the circular brick driveway. Mr. Mendoza, dressed in the typical ranch wear of jeans and cotton shirt, walked over to the car.

"We caught these two," he said after introductions were over. He pointed to two men sitting with their heads down at the side of the yard. Even though they were bound hand and foot, an armed employee stood guard over them. "We made them clean up the trash they left behind. They didn't give us any trouble. None at all."

Brooke looked at the men. Both had bloody scrapes on their faces. Their cheeks were crimson and the skin was broken. Redness near one of the men's eyes was sure to develop into a black eye.

"From the look of their faces, it seems they did." She concluded there were likely more bruises on the covered parts of the men's bodies that would be visible if a physical examination was conducted.

"You know how it is." Mendoza glared at the men.

"Yes, we know exactly how it is," Brooke stared at the armed man until he looked away. "We'll take them now."

73

"I'd like to brand them before you do, so they can be identified if they come back. It might make these people think twice before they show up here again. Maybe then they'll stay on their own side of the river."

"We won't allow that." Darien's voice had a quality that made Mendoza back up a few steps. "That hasn't been legal since slavery times," he added and glared at the rancher.

Mendoza blinked and looked away. "Seems like we can't do nothing about none of this, except pay for repairs out of our own pockets. We hardworking ranchers have to put up with stuff like this too much, and we don't get much help from the patrol." He glared at the two men again.

"We've been a bit busy."

"If you'd keep people like these out of the country, things like those bombs wouldn't happen."

"If you have proof of a connection to anybody, legal or illegal, the patrol would welcome the information." Brooke took a step toward him.

"I don't need no proof. I know what I know."

"Let's get these men to headquarters." Darien's voice caught her attention.

Brooke narrowed her eyes at Mendoza a few seconds, then she led one of the prisoners to the car while Darien took the other.

The ride back to the station was quiet. Brooke kept busy driving within the speed limit rather than taking her anger out on the road.

Lord, please help me remember You are still in charge.

Sitting beside her, Darien closed his hands into fists. The men in the back seat didn't make a sound.

CHAPTER TEN

BROOKE AND DARIEN transferred the prisoners to the guard on duty at the lock-up, then completed their paperwork. Despite his longer legs and lengthy stride, Darien had to work to keep up with Brooke as they walked to the parking lot.

"If we had the proper clothes, I'd suggest we go for a run before we go back on patrol," Darien said as Brooke's quick steps ate up the distance to the car. She turned to face him, leaned against the vehicle, and crossed her arms over her chest. She tapped her heel on the concrete. Darien stood with her.

"If they had a proper gym in this building," she said, "I'd go pound the punching bag and pretend it's Mendoza." She searched Darien's eyes. "He put my religion to the test. I mean it when I say I prayed for the Lord to help me maintain my self-control when we were with that man." She glanced at her watch. "The last thing I feel like doing is getting back in the car and riding for hours." She shook her head. "But we have a long time before our shift is over."

She closed her eyes, and Darien assumed she was praying. When she opened them again, he witnessed the struggle in their deep, angry depths. He figured she was as angry as he was.

"How about we take an early lunch break," Darien said after checking the time. "Any place around here we can go?"

"Good idea." Brooke nodded. "We can try that new soul food restaurant. Ida's is close enough so we can walk, if it's okay with you."

"Sounds fine."

"Good. Maybe by the time we get back, I won't still be tempted to punch out Mendoza's lights," Brooke said as she strode out of the parking lot.

"I hope so," Darien said. "You can't count on me to hold you back."

"You and I would be fighting over who gets to pound him first." Brooke's voice lightened a little.

"You got that right."

Brooke smiled at Darien. "Maybe it wasn't such a good idea for them to partner us. In situations like this, it wouldn't be 'good cop, bad cop.' More likely it would be 'Let's see who can teach the offender a lesson first.' Right?" Her smile widened and a dimple appeared in her left cheek.

"Uh, yeah. Right."

"I'm kidding." Brooke frowned. "I would never hit a person in custody. Not even Mendoza, no matter how tempting that would be."

"I know that."

"Oh. Okay. I wasn't sure. If I did something like that, I'd be just as bad as Mendoza." She glanced at Darien, then away. "Let's cross here. The diner is around the corner and four blocks down. I guess we could have driven, but there's that pent-up anger thing we got going. You okay?"

"Huh?"

"I asked if you're okay with this.'

"Oh. Yeah. Right."

They walked in silence. They spoke to people they passed, but Darien had trouble keeping his mind on work. He was back at where he became aware of her smile.

Darien frowned. *Feels to me like we suddenly got something else going too. Does adrenaline boost testosterone levels, or is it just me?*

He knew he wouldn't find an answer, but he tried to anyway, as he battled his new awareness of Brooke.

Darien had never been in this area of town, so she pointed out various places as they walked. Darien was grateful he didn't have to respond with more than an 'okay' or an 'uh-huh.'

By the time they reached the diner, he had himself under control, and she was back to being his neutral partner, almost.

They ordered their lunches and went to the park across the street to eat. When they were settled on a bench, Darien asked the question that'd been nagging him since they picked up the prisoners.

"What's with Mendoza? Isn't he of Mexican descent?"

"Yeah, but it's a good thing you didn't ask him, or we'd still be there. He would have spent twenty minutes filling you in on his lineage. Short version, his ancestors were here before Texas took this land from Mexico. His people fled oppression further south and settled here. This was still part of Mexico, but it's so far from any government seat that they were left alone. He would be quick to let you know that his ranch was in his family before the Europeans set foot on North America." She looked at him. "He never mentions the people who were here before the Spanish arrived."

"Why does he have such a strong attitude toward illegal immigrants? I realize they do property damage, and I can understand his anger over that, but he acts as if he hates them."

"He says 'these people are a bad element and make it worse for people like me, people who are here legitimately.' His words, not mine." She stared at her sandwich. "I was told that a few years back, he shot immigrants on two different occasions. He drew a lot of heat from each incident, but, despite the fact that it's rare for them to carry guns, the courts couldn't prove that he wasn't acting in self defense as he claimed. It hasn't happened since then. Maybe that last trial shook him." She glanced at Darien. "That judge had a Spanish name too, but he didn't share Mendoza's mindset. I understand he gave him a strong enough warning so that Mendoza hasn't encountered a quote 'armed trespasser' since, and that was six years ago."

They finished eating then went back to the car.

Back on patrol, they didn't encounter anything out of the ordinary, not even a makeshift gate or a cut fence.

"Thank the Lord for a normal routine," Brooke said.

"I agree with that."

When it was time, they checked out and returned home.

THAT EVENING, BROOKE settled in for a couple hours of normal television when the phone rang.

"Just got off duty, and I'm coming over to vent about my new partner," Leah said after Brooke answered the phone. Brooke smiled and waited. Better than anything on television.

Leah arrived twenty minutes later.

After a quick hug, she went into the living room. "My new partner is a trip with a capital 'T.' He had two weeks of foot patrol in town, and now he thinks he's ready to re-write the procedures manual." She stood and paced back and forth in front of the couch. "He thought he had a better way of doing everything. He had the nerve to think he was going to drive." She stopped in front of Brooke, wide-eyed. "Can you imagine that? He'd never been to that part of the area before, yet Mister Man thought he should drive."

"You think it was because he's a man and you're a woman?"

"Who knows? I was nice. I gave him the benefit of the doubt, because if I thought that was the reason it would not have been a pretty scene." She glared and Brooke laughed. "I put up with Mister I-Know-Better-Than-You-Do all morning. Finally, after we broke for lunch, I played my trump card. I used the nine-letter word."

"Nine-letter word?"

"Probation. I reminded Mister Thing that I have a lot to do with his evaluation, and if he didn't get with the program, maybe he'd find himself back at the academy for remedial training."

"Did it work?"

Leah flopped down on the couch. "Oh, yeah. He probably almost bit through the inside of his cheek, but he kept his mouth shut and listened and obeyed orders." She leaned back and laughed. "I'll bet his jaws are sore from keeping his teeth clamped shut for the rest of our shift."

"You're saying that before he's assigned to partner with somebody else, he might need dentures because his teeth will be worn away?"

"Could be. At least we have a good dental plan." Leah laughed, then she glanced at Brooke. "How'd it go with you? Any problems with being in that area again?"

Brooke shook her head. "No. We had a distraction."

"Yeah, I know. You were riding with him."

"Girl, stop it." Brooke frowned. "Remember Mendoza?"

"The guy who forgot about his roots and killed those people a while back?"

"He's the one. We weren't on duty long when we got a call to go to his ranch."

"He didn't kill anyone else, did he?"

"No. This time he had two prisoners." Brooke told what had happened. "Those two were glad to see us, never mind that it meant they'd be sent back." She blinked. "You should have seen the relief in their eyes when they saw our uniforms."

"It's people like that creature Mendoza who almost make you ashamed to be an American." Leah stared at Brooke. "Aside from the encounter with the evil vigilante, how did the shift go with stud muffin?"

"I don't think they use that term any more."

"To paraphrase Shakespeare, a hunk by any other name is still eye candy." She laughed. "So. How did it go?"

"It went as it should have."

"No struggling to fight the feeling? No working hard to keep your mind on work?"

"Leah, you need to stop. You need to get a life."

"I'm trying to, but this crazy schedule is cramping my style. It's messing with my love life."

"What love life?"

"Exactly. How can a sister find Mister Right when she's working crazy hours?"

Brooke laughed. "Since you're my friend, I won't point out that you didn't have one before."

"Like you're not in that same boat with me."

"Hey, I never claimed to have a love life."

"True." Leah stood. "Anyway, now that I vented, I'd better go. You have to get up early."

"Yeah. I wonder how long we'll have ten on and ten off?" Brooke said as they walked to the door.

"I wonder how long it will take us to get used to it. That will probably come sooner than any reduction of duty hours."

"I hate to say it, but I think you're right."

AFTER A RESTLESS night, Brooke woke up on time, but didn't move. Instead, she lay there frowning. How would she ever work with Darien after the dream she'd had about him?

In it, they were in love and planning on a life together forever.

If that was a message from the Lord about what her future held, she wouldn't mind.

It was all Leah's fault. If she hadn't brought Darien up last night, Brooke would have had a normal night's rest. She climbed out of bed, regretting it was all a dream.

Nothing will ever happen between us. It can't. Partners don't get involved. It's against the rules for a reason. All of the focus has to be on the job. The horror of the bomb came back to her.

Even if nobody makes a mistake, terrible things can still happen. I don't want to think about how much worse it could be if the job took second place in attention.

By the time Darien rang her doorbell, Brooke was in professional mode, but it was shaken for a few seconds when she greeted him. He looked just as he had in her dream—handsome, strong, in control.

It's gonna be a struggle to keep that dream away for ten hours, she thought as they got into her car. *I pray I'm up to the task.*

CHAPTER ELEVEN

INSTEAD OF DRIVING straight on Route 281, Brooke varied her driving pattern. She took side roads so Darien could get a feel for the area. Whenever they passed a ranch or farm, she filled him in about the family who owned it. If the landowner was outside, she introduced him. If an incident had occurred at a location, she told him.

When they came to places known as crossing points used by illegal immigrants in the past, she slowed the car. They paid close attention to the areas within a few miles of those spots. History showed that coyotes, those directing illegal immigrants from the Mexican side, didn't bother to move far from where they had met with success.

Twice Brooke and Darien inspected suspicious-looking sections of fencing, but they didn't find anything out of the ordinary.

By the time they broke for lunch, Brooke's dream was still securely locked away where it couldn't interfere with her concentration on the job. If she had her way, it would never come out again. In the back of her mind, though, was the possibility God had other plans.

After lunch they covered the same area, but this time Brooke varied the order and the direction she drove down the streets.

They returned to town by different roads. Regardless of the route they took, the closer they got to town the more of the aftermath of the bombing they encountered. Many cleanup crews remained hard at work.

For the rest of the week, Brooke continued to vary the route. Each day, especially in town, they noted progress made in clearing debris, but it would be a while before things were close to normal.

The alert stayed high, but their shifts were routine. Brooke was all business on duty. After she went home, however, thoughts of Darien nagged her. It didn't help to have Leah comment on him whenever they talked.

By the end of the second week of the new schedule, Darien was familiar with the route and had met all the ranchers and farmers in the area.

The third week, he drove. They alternated the next two weeks. The only undocumented visitors captured in the area during that time were apprehended by officers at several of the checkpoints. The captives posed no threat to national security according to daily reports.

Brownsville, as in other areas of the United States, settled into a peace of sorts, but it was as if the entire country was waiting for another big hit.

During casual conversations while riding on duty, Brooke and Darien shared information about their families. Soon, it was as if they'd known each other a long time. She wondered if he felt the same way.

Neither mentioned the possibility of being assigned new partners, but it would come. A new class was graduating from the academy in a few weeks. Additional training was taking place for National Guard members and the reserves who would be assigned to the area. Trainers from the Border Patrol Academy were temporarily assigned to military bases all over the country to ensure those undergoing special training would be ready for deployment along the border. Rumors flitted through the ranks. Everybody knew transfers were coming, but not exactly when. Brooke and Darien suspected their days together as partners would soon end.

Two weeks later, at the end of their shift, Brooke and Darien were ordered to report for a briefing with Director Young. She was glad he was all right and back to work.

As she walked down the hall, Brooke wished it was shorter so this could be over. But then she also wished it was longer so the change wouldn't take place. She was used to Darien.

When they reached the outer office, they joined a few dozen agents waiting in the hall. It looked as if a lot of shuffling of personnel was about to take place. Brooke and Darien reported to the guard at the door and were allowed entry.

"We have enough new personnel in place to make changes," Commander Young said after he greeted the group. He looked at Darien. "Officer McKee, you've been patrolling your assigned area for weeks. Are you familiar enough with it to break in a new partner?"

"Yes, sir." Darien didn't give any indication of his feelings about the imminent change. He looked as if it didn't matter to him at all.

"Good." Commander Young looked at Brooke. "Looks like you get a new partner too."

"Yes, sir." She tried not to feel disappointment.

The Commander gave an order through the intercom. Almost immediately there was a tap on his door and two men came in.

They looked young enough to be new graduates from one of the academies rather than experienced agents transferred from other sectors. For certain they weren't National Guard or members of the reserves—not enough time had passed for the additional training.

Commander Young introduced Brooke and Darien to their new partners, and assigned them to areas. He dismissed them after informing them their duty would start in the morning.

To Brooke, it didn't seem as if any time had passed before she and Darien were walking down the hall, talking with new partners. She overheard Darien and his partner discussing going over to the cafeteria for coffee so they could talk, and she felt left out. She wouldn't have any more coffee breaks, or lunches, or anything else with Darien. From now on they would be former partners and neighbors, nothing more.

She suggested to her new partner, Alonzo Keating, that they do the same so they could get acquainted.

"Not necessary." He shook his head. "I'm a quick study. It's been a busy week since I got here, and I haven't had much time to spend with my lady. Now that I have my partner, my assignment, and my duty schedule, the two of us can relax and get reacquainted, if you know what I mean. Chill." He grinned. "Where we gonna meet in the morning?"

"Inside headquarters. I'll wait for you at the desk fifteen minutes before we go on duty."

"I'll do my best to get there by then, but I have to come from across town. I don't suppose you want to pick me up? That way my lady can use the car." Again, he grinned. Brooke guessed perhaps that smile let him get his way too many times, probably with women. Not this one. She used a killer smile of her own.

"Your *lady* can drop you off. I expect to be driving from the lot no more than two minutes after we sign in for duty."

"You always that precise?"

Her smile was super sweet. "When it comes to work, yes. See you in the morning."

She left him standing on the sidewalk. Maybe he was waiting for 'his lady.' Maybe not. Brooke didn't care. That had nothing to do with her. As long as he did his job and kept his mind on work when they were on duty, she didn't care about his private life.

She walked home since Darien drove this morning. She sighed. It would be strange not to leave the apartment complex riding together when they went on duty tomorrow or any day after that.

She cut through the university campus, lonely not to have company. *Get used to it. He was your partner.* She crossed the little foot bridge over the stream. *Nothing else. Now he's just your neighbor.*

When she reached the complex, she stopped and glanced toward Darien's apartment. Then she went up to her own.

A few hours later, a knock on the door pulled Brooke from cooking dinner.

"Hi, ex-partner," Darien said when the door opened.

"Hi, yourself." Brooke grinned. "Come on in. I'm frying some chicken." She shrugged. "I know it's not the healthiest way to cook it, but I need some comfort food after meeting Mister-All-That-And-So-Much-More Keating."

"That bad, huh?" Darien grinned as he followed her to the kitchen.

"I know I only spent a few minutes with him, but Officer Keating doesn't make a good first impression. Whether it's that he doesn't have a clue, or that he doesn't care, I don't know, and it doesn't make a difference. I feel I am in for trying times." Brooke turned her attention back to the stove.

"Are you saying that he's no Darien?" He chuckled as he set the table.

She glanced at him. "I have the feeling there's only one of those."

Their stares held for a long while before the lid on the pot of vegetables clattered and broke the connection.

"Funny," he said. "I have the same feeling about finding another Brooke."

"Will you please get the salad from the refrigerator?" she asked after a long pause.

"Sure thing," he answered. Neither moved.

The chicken sizzling broke through her fog, and she turned her attention to it.

Neither said a word as she lifted the meat onto paper towels to drain, patted it, and removed the towels from the plate. Behind her, she heard the refrigerator door finally open as Darien took out the salad and the dressing and set them on the table.

Still silent, Brooke made gravy to go with the rice cooking in the microwave. The only sound was of them moving around. That noise was interrupted by a ding of the microwave.

Darien retrieved the potholders and put the rice on the table. Brooke poured the gravy into a container and placed it on the table. It felt natural for them to be working together in the kitchen.

"What do you want to drink? Coffee? Sweet tea?" She avoided looking at him directly.

"I don't need anything else to disturb my sleep. Ice water is good."

Brooke refused to question his statement about disturbed sleep. She had her own experience to remember. Taking the safe way out, she refused to look at his face. She took her seat and said grace.

As they filled their plates, neither mentioned the flirty words between them, although the simple sentences lay between them like flowers cast aside.

"Tell me about *your* new partner." She congratulated herself on finding a safe, neutral subject.

"Jack is okay. He's the opposite of your Alonzo."

"He's not *my* Alonzo," Brooke quickly pointed out.

"You know what I mean." Darien laughed. "Besides he *is* yours during your shift." He ate a bite of chicken. "Hey, this is kickin'."

"Why do you sound so surprised? You've tasted my cooking before."

"You *baked* the chicken before. This goes straight back to my roots and my grandmama's Sunday dinners. It was worth sitting through the six hour church service to get it."

"Six hours? No way."

"It sure felt like it at the time." He grinned. "Anyway, we went home to a meal of her famous fried chicken, greens, candied yams, and cornbread. And for dessert, we had her famous peach cobbler." He shook his head. "Man, my mouth waters just thinking about it."

"After hearing that story, I'm flattered at the comparison of my chicken to hers." She laughed. "My mom had to practically drag me into the kitchen to get me to learn how to cook. I would much rather be hanging with my friends and maybe jumping Double Dutch."

"Whoa. Who would name their kid 'Double Dutch' and why were you jumping him? Or her? You don't strike me as a bully. Was this a girl gang you ran with?" He frowned at her as she began laughing. "What? Those are simple questions. And there's nothing funny about a gang of kids jumping another kid."

88

"It's..." Brooke laughed harder as Darien continued to stare. "Okay, okay," she said as she wiped her eyes and took a deep breath. "I forgot you're a country boy." She still grinned wide. "Let me educate you a bit about the East Coast life, especially in the northeast." Her shoulders shook as she giggled. Then she took another deep breath. "What we have here is a serious cultural gap."

"I'd educate you about the pluses of country living, but I'll save it. I want to hear your explanation."

"Let me fill you in. First, I never met anybody named 'Double Dutch.' I've heard a lot of strange names, but nothing like that." She giggled, put on a straight face, then giggled again. "Double Dutch is a way of jumping rope." She leaned forward. "You turn two ropes at the same time in opposite directions. You can have teams. The routines can be quite intricate. There are even Double Dutch contests. One year Gail, Trish, Lakita, and I made it to the semi-finals in New York. Of course, everybody in the hood thought we should have won. We thought so too." She sighed. "Man, we spent so many hours perfecting our routine."

She shook her head. "And my 'girl gang members' were at the top of the class all through school. We graduated one, two, three, and four. But I digress. Let's get back to your partner."

"Jack's back should be sore from all the bowing and scraping he does. The man almost asks which hand he should use to open the door. He's like a kindergarten kid on the first day of school."

"Think we can figure out a way to combine them, mix them up, then divide them? That would give us two normal partners."

"If we could do that, people would be coming forth with a whole lot of other ideas for the application."

They finished the meal and the conversation remained neutral. Brooke was thankful for that.

"That was delicious." Darien set his napkin down. "I don't suppose I can expect peach cobbler for dessert?"

"Ida probably has some at her restaurant, but you wouldn't want to go that far."

"Not for cobbler." His gaze was steady on her. "What are we gonna do?" he asked. His smile was gone.

"I don't know." She didn't pretend not to know what he was talking about. She shrugged. "Take it slow and wait for a sign from the Lord."

"I guess that's best, but life is so short."

"Yes."

Brooke thought of the bombings. Darien looked as if his thoughts were in the same place. Neither mentioned it. The tragedy was big enough where it was, without dragging it out into the light. Finally, Brooke stood and stacked the plates. Darien followed suit and gathered the tableware.

As they cleaned up after the meal, they talked about unimportant things. Finally, the kitchen gleamed.

"One good thing about not being partners—no worries about complications," Darien said.

"Yes." They walked to the door.

"My turn to cook tomorrow. Okay?"

"Okay. Should I expect peach cobbler?"

"Sure." He nodded. "I can stop by Ida's and get some on the way home."

They laughed, but it faded, leaving them standing at the door staring at each other. Darien leaned close, and she swayed toward him, but he pulled back before their lips touched. "Take it slow. Right." He smiled and nodded. "See you tomorrow?"

"Oh. Yeah. Yeah. Tomorrow."

After he had gone, Brooke stood in the hallway frowning at the door. Then she went about closing the house down for the night.

No sense fighting it, she thought as she entered her bedroom. *It is what it is and will be what the Lord wills it to be.*

CHAPTER TWELVE

"I DON'T KNOW why I'm so nervous," Brooke muttered as she stood outside the door to Darien's apartment. *Sure you do,* her mind responded. *You know things turned a corner between you two last night. It's natural to be apprehensive when facing the unknown. Cool it. Just trust in the Lord.* She frowned.

"Thank you for that, Ms. Freud," she muttered and knocked on the door. *Not only am I psychoanalyzing myself, I'm giving advice too.*

Darien opened the door as if he had been standing on the other side waiting for her arrival. "Hi, come on in."

His smile sent flutters through her. She didn't need to analyze the reason for that.

Leftovers at home would have been a lot safer, she thought as she followed him into his home. *But you can miss a lot of good things if you always play it safe,* she told herself. *You could miss a blessing from God.*

"I would have fixed some appetizers, but I didn't want to set the bar too high for the rest of the male population." He grinned.

"So I went right to dinner. Next time, I'll add the appetizers. Come on out to the kitchen."

"Next time?"

"Yeah. I figured if I use the tableware correctly, don't eat my collards with my hands, don't wipe my mouth on my sleeve or do something else equally disgusting, this might not be a one-time event."

"This is an event?"

"Feels like it to me." His stare held hers for a long minute.

She cleared her throat. "Not having appetizers is okay. Lunch was a long time ago, so it's good to get right to dinner and not fill up on something else first."

His smile softened when she changed the subject. "Have a seat," he told her when they reached the table.

"Okay, but no fair. You did my job."

"Your job?"

"Yeah. You already set the table."

"Oh, right. You can do the honor next time," he said with a wider grin.

"There's that next time thing again," Brooke said as she sat in the chair he pulled out.

"I'm encouraging that seed to grow."

"That's what you call it, huh?"

"That or doggedness, persistence, stubbornness. Take your pick. They all fit this situation." He stared down at her for the longest second Brooke had ever experienced.

"So. How was your day?" Darien asked. He set the salad bowl on the table, then quickly put the rest of the meal in place.

"Wow," Brooke said she examined at the variety of food in the serving dishes. "I am impressed."

"And well you should be," Darien said as he sat opposite her. "The yams were easy to find, although I did have to candy them. The collards were something else. I had to ask Miss Ida for help in locating them." His grin took on an almost boyish quality. "She was reluctant to reveal her source."

"But you used your charm on her." Brooke wished she could take the words back after she saw the expression on Darien's face.

"You think I have charm?" He leaned his elbows on the table. His gaze twinkled.

"Get back to Miss Ida and the greens."

"Okay. I'll let that charm comment slide for now. Anyway, I had to swear on the grave of my dog, Snoopy, that this is a special occasion, and I will still come to her restaurant on a regular basis and eat more than my share of collard greens." He nodded toward the dishes. "Go ahead. Help yourself. I didn't slave over a hot stove for you to let my creations get cold." When, instead of reaching for the food, Brooke continued to frown, he put yams and greens on her plate. He finished by adding a portion of short ribs.

"Your dog, Snoopy?"

"Another story for another time." Grin still in place, he nodded. "Yep. I had to go through a lot to put this meal on the table, but if you're impressed, it's worth it." He reached for his fork, but she took his hand. She gave thanks to the Lord, then let it go. He looked embarrassed, but didn't say anything.

"I'm greatly impressed. That story about the greens was very good, even without hearing about your dog." Brooke held up a forkful of collards, then tasted them. "Umm. Wow. These are excellent."

"Thank you, ma'am." He bowed his head slightly, then served his own plate.

"These short ribs are way past delicious too." Brooke took a bite and chewed. "As Grandmom Jane used to say, 'It tastes like you really put your foot in the pot.'" She frowned. "I have no idea what that means and the concept is disgusting, but that's the expression she used whenever she tasted something delicious that somebody else cooked." Brooke grinned as she took a bite of yams. "This is 'off the hook.'" She shrugged. "Or off the chain. Whichever. Both fit."

"I'm just glad you like it. I aim to please."

"Oh. I'm pleased."

"I'm glad I could give you pleasure." They stopped eating and just looked at each other. They both knew they weren't talking about food anymore. Finally, Brooke cleared her throat and glanced down at the table before looking back at him.

"So. How was your day?"

"I asked you that first, and you didn't answer."

"Oh. Sorry. One bite of your food, and my taste buds took over and shoved your question aside." She gave a weak grin. "About like yesterday. Alonzo is a throwback, a chauvinistic pig. I won't press the 'pig' part considering our jobs, but the chauvinistic label was made for him. First, he headed for the driver's seat."

"Did he know which area you were going to patrol? Was he familiar with it?"

"A little thing like lack of knowledge doesn't stop somebody who was at the top of his class at the academy."

"He told you that?"

"Several times in several ways. He reminded me again as he asked for the key—to my car."

"Since you couldn't fire him, what did you do?"

"I informed him that if he was riding with me, he was *riding* with me, and I didn't care if he graduated number one from every institution he could name, he wasn't driving until *I* decided." She

95

shook her head. "We hadn't even gotten in the car, and already we were bumping heads. If somebody from one of the wanted posters in headquarters had come up to us in the parking lot and carried on a long conversation, Alonzo and I wouldn't have been focused enough to grab him." She sighed. "That man is going to get us in trouble. Big time." She frowned.

"I hope not."

"Not as much as I do."

"I don't know about that."

His concerned expression spoke volumes.

She stared at her fork as if she couldn't remember if she was bringing the food to her mouth or putting the fork on her plate. Finally, she cleared her throat again.

"Your turn. How was your day?"

"Brooke, you know something is going on between us. I don't know when it started, but I do know that it started." He hesitated. "I don't know where it's going, but I'd like to find out." His gaze remained steady, examining her. "I hope you do too." He paused again. "If not, I'll try to back off."

Brooke looked away, considered his words, then returned her gaze to his.

"I feel it too," she admitted, "and I find it unsettling." She frowned. "In college I was known for over-planning. I prepared for every possible scenario in any given situation. This thing..." She sighed. "It frightens me. It's...it's like jumping off a diving board and not knowing how deep the water below is." She frowned. "I know I face the unknown every time I go on patrol, but this is different. I don't have a way to prepare for this."

"No need to be scared." His face softened. "You can set the pace, and I'll follow your lead. Okay?" His voice hovered close to a whisper.

Brooke hesitated, then nodded. "Okay," she said. "What?" she asked when Darien wiped his forehead in an exaggerated gesture.

"I didn't know how you would react when I said that. I was afraid you'd turn me down. That I wanted it so badly I feared your attraction was only in my imagination."

"No, it's not. After the madness settled down, I noticed you. Of course, Leah's comment was the trigger."

"Leah? Your friend you introduced me to?"

"One and the same."

"What did she say?"

"I'm not telling. It might give you a big head."

"Aw, come on. You got me curious, now."

"Too bad. She probably didn't say anything the girls in high school and college didn't tell you." Brooke's grin spread across her face. She leaned closer and stared slowly at each feature of his face. "With you it probably started in grade school."

"You agreed with her, right? It was something positive, I hope."

"So, how was your day?" Brooke grinned as she changed the subject.

Darien chuckled. "Okay, I'll back off, but I want you to know I'm keeping count of the times I cut you some slack. Now, getting back to my partner. If I had heard one more 'sir,' the force would be minus a team. He'd be dead, and I'd be in jail or in psychiatric care."

"Sir?"

"Yeah. As in 'yes, sir' and 'no, sir' and 'sorry, sir', and 'I don't know, sir.'" Darien leaned against the back of his chair. "After a while I found myself gripping the steering wheel so tightly my fingers probably left dents in it. That's okay, though. Better the steering wheel than his neck."

"You think we were that bad when we started out?"

"Of course not. Most new officers are within the normal range. You and I just got the extreme. Sort of like Murphy's Law decided to hone in on us."

"Well, let's hope there are only two of them like that. Of course, Leah got a real winner too." She shook her head. "The patrol is too thin to have any agents who can't fit in, especially given the times. Not being able to take the initiative without direct orders in a tight situation, or going off without thinking things through, can both lead to real trouble."

"That's true."

"Back to your gourmet cooking." Brooke set her fork on her plate. "That meal was fantastic." She sighed. "I ate way too much." She patted her middle. "Many more meals like this, and I won't be able to chase anybody."

"You have a long way to go before you reach that point." His eyes were intense. "And if it happens, you'll take a desk job and be there when I sign off duty, so I'll still get to see you."

"You'd still look for me?"

"No question about it. There'd just be more of you for me."

"Let me help you clean up." Brooke stood and stacked the plates.

"You're very good at that."

"What?"

"Changing the subject."

"Evidently not good enough, since you always catch it."

"Hey, that's because I'm good too." He stood. "However, you have to sit back down. We haven't had dessert yet."

"Dessert? You made dessert?"

"Oh, yeah. Hey, don't be so surprised. I was torn between peach cobbler and banana pudding. Because of time, banana pudding won out. We'll have cobbler another time. Okay?"

"Okay," she said.

Brooke watched him get the casserole from the refrigerator and set it on the table. Her gaze followed him as he retrieved dessert plates. She no longer experienced apprehension about her attraction toward him. Instead, a sense of calm washed over her.

I'm not sure where this thing between us is going nor when it will get there, but I have to go along with it. I feel God's hand on it.

CHAPTER THIRTEEN

BROOKE AND DARIEN fell into a pattern of sharing evening meals over the next three weeks. Neither dwelled on the growing attraction between them, but that didn't mean it didn't exist. Instead, they kept things neutral on the outside while trying to ignore what was developing inside.

They discussed their day's work, sharing the good as well as the bad. Unfortunately for Brooke, she had more bad to share.

"I'm sorry I'm late. I'm afraid I'm going to kill that man if he doesn't get us killed first." Brooke slammed the door and whirled around to face Darien when he let her in one evening.

"Hello."

"Oh. Sorry. Hi, Darien." She frowned, but he knew it wasn't because of him.

"What did your partner do today?"

"That man." She shook her head. "I should be cooking tonight," she continued as if she hadn't heard Darien's question. "I wouldn't even need to light the stove. I've got enough heat right now to cook for the entire population of Brownsville just by holding the food in my palms." She waved her hands as if she expected Darien to see fire coming from them. "I spent almost the entire shift asking the Lord to give me patience and to guide me in how I handled things. If He wasn't God, He would have gotten sick of me."

"It's too late for you to cook. I already did. Come on out to the kitchen, and you can tell me all about it before you erupt."

Her footsteps were so loud that Darien didn't have to look to see if she was behind him.

She walked to the cupboard to pull down plates, but turned to face Darien without opening the door. Instead, she crossed her arms over her chest.

"What did he do today?" Darien repeated.

"I was stupid enough to let him drive, so I guess I have to take some of the blame, but really, he should be ready for that by now." She released a hard breath. "Anyway, we were all right for a while, and I was beginning to think he made progress." She leaned back against the counter and shook her head. "I still can't believe it happened."

"What?"

"We pulled up behind a car on Palm Boulevard. You know, on the other side of Amigoland Mall going north? Anyway, the car in front of us was weighted down." She glanced at Darien. "They could have been carrying anything—drugs, guns, a body. Anything. So I told Alonzo to ease off while I called for back-up." Brooke began to pace the small area between the counter and the table.

"I take it he didn't?"

"You got it in one. You've heard the expression 'fools rush in?' If there's an illustration of that saying anywhere, the picture has Alonzo's face." She glared. "Anyway, the car drove around to the back of the mall. We were waiting for back-up, as per procedure in cases like this. At least I was waiting. Mr. Hot Shot decided to make a move when the driver stopped the car. Alonzo didn't even turn off the engine before he jumped out of the car, *my* car I might add, and ran toward the other vehicle. The driver ran inside the service entrance door. I was so tempted to let Alonzo go alone while I stayed with the vehicle."

"You followed him?"

"I couldn't leave *El Stupido* in there alone. Too much paperwork to fill out if you lose a partner. Besides, at that point I wanted to kill him myself." She glanced at Darien. "So, yeah, I followed him inside." She stopped, then went back to pacing. "Anyway, the driver was nowhere in sight and there were six doors leading off from the dark hallway."

Brooke stopped pacing. "I watched as my dumb partner tried each door. The third opened, and he went inside." She glanced at Darien again. "There's that fool-in-a-hurry thing again. By the time I got inside, Alonzo had the guy backed against the wall. Three other people were watching. From behind Alonzo." She walked a few steps away, then back. "Any one of them could have killed him, and they could have all scattered, and we never would have found the killer. If I survived, that is."

"You took the guy in?"

"Uh-uh. Not right then." She shrugged. "The man showed proof that he's a citizen, so no problem there. We asked him why he ran, and he said that he owes somebody some money and he thought we were after him for that."

"You believed him?"

"No, but he's a citizen, and we had no proof that he did anything wrong."

"What'd you do?"

"I didn't do what I wanted to do. Instead, I ordered Alonzo back outside. We made the guy go with us. I still planned to wait for instructions pertaining to the man's car."

"The car was empty when you got there."

"Uh-uh." She visibly tightened her jaw. "Better than that. His car was gone. I swear he looked relieved, but he accused us of being responsible for his car being stolen. We pointed out that he had passengers in the car. He said he had been nice and picked up the three men who were strangers and gave them a ride because it was so hot walking. He also said his car would have been all right if we hadn't chased him from it. We couldn't prove anything different."

"What do you think was in the car?"

"I *hope* he just had a couple of illegal immigrants hiding under the seats, in a false bottom, or in the trunk. That area is so vulnerable and all of those means of smuggling have been uncovered by agents." She shook her head. "I don't want to consider that drugs, explosives, or weapons might have been his cargo." She seemed lost in thought. Darien figured the bombing of headquarters was on her mind.

"You took the guy in."

"We had to. He insisted on it. Can you believe it? He had to report a stolen car and didn't have any way to get to headquarters, remember? The guy talked the whole time about how much he needed his car to go back and forth to work, and he thought the Border Patrol owed him one. I kept quiet until we took him in, but if I had my way Alonzo and his lady would be walking and the guy would have a replacement car." She threw up her hands.

"Sounds fair to me."

"We did the paperwork on the stolen car incident and left the office. I know I'll hear from the commander about this. I'm the senior officer of the team. When you follow procedures, nothing like that should happen."

"That's all you reported? The chase that led to the stolen car? Nothing about Alonzo's actions?"

"Not then. Alonzo said he was sorry. Then he had the nerve to walk away from me and leave the building. I let him get as far as the outside steps before I stopped him. Do you know he actually asked if we had to go back out on patrol since it was almost time to clock out? He said we'd be late getting back if we went all the way out there and had to return." Her eyes widened. "He thought that was the end of it, that his little 'sorry' erased his behavior. I ordered him to the car even though what I wanted to do was ream him out in front of anyone who was within shouting distance."

"Wasn't his lady coming for him?"

"I didn't care if the First Lady, the President, and a whole entourage was coming. As soon as we got into the car, he started talking. He swore he realized what he did was wrong, and he wouldn't do it again. He tried to convince me that there wasn't anything to write up about his actions, since the guy was legit and the only thing that happened was a stolen car."

"You convinced him otherwise." Darien smiled.

"I asked him if he wanted me to turn in my version alone. He decided to write his report. *After* we finished patrolling."

"You signed off on it?"

"I added my version. Since reports state facts only and not opinions, when you read them you can't get the feel for the seriousness of the situation he put us in." She shook her head. "I sure hope I got through to him, though, for both our sakes."

"So do I." He placed his hands on her shoulders. "I don't want to lose you."

104

Brooke stared at him a few seconds. Finally, she answered. "That makes two of us."

"We haven't even had a chance to do this."

"What?" Brooke's voice was weak.

"This."

He drew her close. Then he captured her mouth with his. The contact was barely there at first. Then the pressure increased from both of them.

Brooke's hands brushed across his shoulders and her arms found the way around his neck .

The kiss went on forever, but not long enough.

Darien eased away from her, but kept his hands on her arms. They stared into each other's eyes for a few seconds. Then Darien spoke. "I think we should send Alonzo a thank-you note," Darien whispered against Brooke's ear before he nuzzled it.

"Yeah?" Brooke's voice was soft.

"Um-hmm." Darien kissed her cheek. "If he hadn't made you so angry, you wouldn't have forgotten to close the gate to the fence you've placed between us." He kissed the corner of her mouth, then pulled back.

"Probably true." She pressed her mouth to his jaw, then trailed a finger along the side. Then she pulled back too.

They stood that way for a few seconds. Then, by unspoken agreement, they separated. Brooke cleared her throat.

"So. How was *your* day?" She looked at him with wide-eyed innocence.

"Not as eventful as yours." Darien forced a serious look onto his face. Then they both laughed. "I'll tell you about it while we eat."

As they enjoyed their meal, Darien explained how Jack was adjusting. Conversation danced around the food, but it never touched on the moment they'd just shared.

They finished eating, the kitchen was as clean as it had been since Darien moved in, and it was after eleven.

Brooke looked around. "I'd better go."

"Yeah." Darien walked over to her. He wrapped his arm around her waist and they walked to the door.

"Goodnight." Brooke turned to face him.

"Yeah."

"I'd better go," Brooke said.

"Yeah," Darien agreed. He touched her lips with his and pulled away. Then, with one hand still around her waist, he opened the door with the other.

"Goodnight."

"I'll walk you home."

"I'm just down the complex."

"Can't be too careful these days. Besides, that way I get to kiss you goodnight all over again." He grinned, then pecked her cheek.

"You have a point."

They walked the few yards to her apartment. Darien kissed her once more and waited until she went inside.

Brooke leaned against the closed door and smiled at the change in their relationship. She was ready for whatever the Lord had in store.

CHAPTER FOURTEEN

BROOKE AWOKE THE next morning smiling. She'd dreamt about Darien again, the same as before. She turned onto her back and opened her eyes. They kissed last night. For real. Not in a dream.

She should get up. Instead, she hit the snooze button, but didn't try to go back to sleep. She folded her hands behind her head, sighed, and stared at the ceiling as if there was something more interesting to look at than the short crack present when she moved in.

When the buzzer went off again, she rose, still smiling, and started preparing to report for duty. Last night, she and Darien had definitely turned a corner in their relationship, and that was all right with her. This felt so right. It must be what the Lord intended.

As she went out the door, she doubted her partner, even if he did something dumber than yesterday, would bring her down.

She slid into her car. She hoped nothing would happen to prove her wrong.

Alonzo followed procedure and didn't question her once, nor did he suggest a better way to do anything. Brooke's mellow mood didn't interfere with her paying attention to her surroundings as they patrolled.

During the next few weeks, Brooke and Darien's goodbye kiss was joined by a welcoming kiss at the door. Each day, their embraces grew deeper and more heated, but at the end of the evening they each went to their own bed alone. They were satisfied to let the relationship progress to the inevitable stage in its own time. No need to rush. If what they had was real, time wouldn't make it lessen.

One day she made a request after dinner. "Will you go to church with me Sunday morning?" She tensed as she waited for his answer. The scripture about being evenly-yoked was on her mind.

"Church service with you?"

"Yes."

"It's been so long. I don't know." He frowned.

"There's no expiration date on worshipping," she said. "It's open-ended. The Lord is always there."

"This is that important to you."

"Very much so."

"I guess it won't hurt."

"I never heard of it doing that." She smiled. "Try it. You might like it."

"I'm on duty next Sunday, but I'll go with you next time we're both off on Sunday."

"Thank you, Darien." She kissed his cheek. "This means a lot to me."

A WEEK LATER, they attended church together. Brooke introduced him to her pastor, Reverend James, who greeted him warmly as she

108

knew he would. When they left, Darien seemed more relaxed than when they arrived.

Over the next weeks, Brooke gave thanks that their time on duty, and the business of the entire Border Patrol Department, remained peaceful. Several teams arrested undocumented immigrants, but that was usual. None of those apprehended was deemed to be a threat to national security. The homeland security rating dropped a notch and everybody relaxed a bit. It was as if time was giving them space to heal and return to normal.

What happened that terrible day left the headlines, but Brooke and everybody in the department knew investigations were ongoing.

Alonzo occasionally questioned Brooke's decisions, but for the most part he followed her directions. She held hope that, by the time his probation was over, he'd be an asset to the department. They needed him and a lot more good agents.

Brooke and Darien continued to share their evening meal and attend church together when both enjoyed a Sunday off. Their conversations, when they discussed their day, showed Darien felt the same about the progress of his partner, Jack, as Brooke felt about Alonzo.

"Looks as if those two will be able to help ease the deficit in the department," Darien said one evening. He and Brooke sat on his sofa, his hand around her shoulder. The television played, but neither paid attention to the program.

"Leah said her partner is working out okay too." Brooke fiddled with the fingers on Darien's other hand. "I heard that, so far, very few of the latest group will need additional training, and that's not because standards have been lowered."

"With the new class at the academy well on their way to graduation, it looks as if the government will be in better shape than it has been in a long time."

"The patrol is still hurting from the hits we took. We needed for something to go our way, and God has blessed us." Brooke glanced at her watch. "I'd better leave. Morning comes early." She stood.

"Not as early as it would if we spent the night together."

Brooke took a deep breath. "I...I should have brought this up before. I might be in the minority." She swallowed hard. "I can't do that. Not outside marriage. I...I probably wasted your time. I should have brought up my belief before." She turned to go, but he put his hand on her arm.

"Hey, don't dump me yet. You know what they say—anything worth having is worth waiting for." He brushed his finger down the side of her face. "Or is 'Good things come to he who waits' better?" He leaned closer and kissed her cheek lightly, then took a step back and looked down into her face. "We'll follow your timetable. What we have is special."

Brooke felt as if a weight had been lifted. He wasn't breaking things off because of her beliefs. She smiled.

Darien opened the door, placed a gentle kiss on Brooke's mouth, and they left his apartment.

"You know this is ridiculous, don't you?" she asked when they reached her apartment less than a minute later. "You can see my door from yours." She handed him her key, and he opened the door.

"We go through this every time you come over. A gentleman walks a lady to her door. My mama and daddy both taught me that." He grinned down at her. "Besides, the gentleman in question gets another kiss." He winked. "They didn't teach me that part. I added it myself." He wrapped his arms around her and kissed her.

"There," he said as he slowly released her. "That should hold you until tomorrow evening," he repeated the phrase he used each time. "Stay safe tomorrow."

"I will if you will." Brooke smiled as she closed the door. After she clicked the lock, she listened to Darien walk away.

The next evening, Brooke stopped by Ida's, bought a peach cobbler and some cooked collards, then hurried home. She went straight into the kitchen and put the chicken on before she changed out of her uniform.

When she returned to the kitchen, she turned on the radio and let the music keep her company until her real company arrived. She smiled as she thought of Darien.

She stirred the chicken stewing on the back of the stove, glanced at the clock, then slid the dumplings into the pot with the chicken. She hesitated, then put the homemade biscuits into the oven. Darien would be there soon.

A short while later, she turned off the stove. The residual heat could finish the biscuits and warm the cobbler. All she had to do was wait for him. She looked at the clock and frowned. He was late.

"A special news bulletin just in," the DJ broke in before the song she was playing ended. "We're taking you live to Border Patrol Headquarters."

Brooke ran to the television and turned it on.

"...we'll give details of this unfolding story as soon as we get them, but what we know so far is this—two Border Patrol officers were shot after stopping a vehicle on Route 77. One was killed and the other is in critical condition. The two men in the vehicle in question were killed and a third is in custody in what was described by a witness as 'a shootout with more bullets flying than he could count.' What should have been a routine stop turned deadly. The man in custody is believed to be Manuel Lomita, the reputed head of the drug cartel that has moved into Reynosa, Mexico, from Colombia. Our government, as well as that of Mexico, has been after him for a long time." The reporter paused. "The names of the two officers have not been released pending notification of next of kin. We'll broadcast further information as soon as we receive it. This is Carlos Westwood, reporting outside Border Patrol Headquarters located in the National Guard Armory in Brownsville, Texas."

The screen went dark, then, after two commercials, the talk show that'd been interrupted resumed as if nothing unusual had happened, as if Brooke's world might not have been shattered.

She stared at the television, but she wasn't seeing the talk show.

"No. Oh, no," she sobbed as she shook her head. "Please, Lord, no." Then, trembling, she tore out the door and dashed to Darien's apartment.

"Darien," she yelled as she pounded on his door, willing him to be there. "Open the door. Please open the door." She sobbed as she continued to hit the door with the palm of her hand. "Please be okay. You have to be okay."

The door opened and Darien, wearing a robe, frowned down at her. Brooke grabbed him and wrapped her arms around his torso and held him tightly.

"What is it, baby?" Darien asked as Brooke tightened her hold on him even more. She rested her head against his chest and brushed her hands back and forth across it as if to make sure he was really there. "Hey, baby. What's wrong?"

"You're okay. You're okay. Thank God, you're okay."

"Yeah." Still frowning, he nodded slowly as he drew her inside the apartment and closed the door. "What happened?" He framed her face with his hand. "What's the matter?"

"You haven't turned on the radio or television since you got home?"

112

"No. I was running a little late so I jumped in the shower as soon as I got in. I didn't want to make you wait." He brushed her hair back from her face. Then he walked her over to the television and turned to the all-news station. Brooke held tightly to his hand.

It was a different reporter, but the news was the same as when Brooke watched. They stood in silence. When the same information was repeated, Darien turned off the set and turned to face Brooke.

"I...I..." She struggled to breathe. "You..." She shook her head. "I thought it was you." Her words were low. "I was afraid it was you." She sobbed. "I was so afraid that your team was the one involved. I know you patrol that area." She swallowed hard. "Oh, Darien." She gripped his arms again. "I don't know what I would do if anything happened to you."

"It's okay, baby. I'm okay." He brushed a thumb through the tears on her cheek. "I'm like that bad penny they talk about. I'll always turn up. I promise." He kissed her where his thumb had brushed. "Okay?"

She drew a ragged breath. "Life is so uncertain. The events of the past few months have taught me that. And then today..." Brooke released a heavy breath as she wiped her face.

"We've all learned that lesson."

"I feel so stupid." She glanced at the floor and shook her head again. She grinned slightly. "I...I really lost it when I thought something happened to you."

"I'm flattered." Darien lifted her face and looked into her eyes. He brushed her tears away with a finger.

"Why do you sound surprised?" A puzzled look covered her face. "You know how I feel about you. You must realize."

"A guy likes to know that it's not one-sided."

She frowned at him. "How could you even think that?"

"I want this between us so much that it's hard for me to tell what's real and what's my imagination anymore," he said. "That's what you do to me." He grinned. "I was just fine on my own and then you came along."

"What we have is real. I know it deep inside." Brooke placed her hands on the sides of his face and brought his mouth down on hers.

Their kiss was full of promises and went on and on. Then Darien eased away.

"I think we should back off." He took a step back. "I don't want us to do something you'll regret later. I don't want us to rush into anything because of what could've happened to me today. I don't want the pleasure of making love with you one time to ruin any chance we might have for a future together."

"Makes sense." Brooke released a long, slow breath. "Get dressed and come on over for dinner. Okay?" she said.

"Okay."

"Don't take too long or things will get cold."

"Cooling off might be a good thing right now."

"True," she said. She smiled as he left.

DARIEN'S THOUGHTS WHIRLED after Brooke left. *This must be what love feels like.* In the past, the very idea of that emotion frightened him. To be committed to an uncertain future with someone seemed foolish. Now, with Brooke, it seemed natural. Normal. He felt relieved. He wanted to spend forever with her.

He went into his bedroom to change. He missed her already.

BROOKE HEADED RIGHT into the kitchen. She just left Darien's, so she knew he was coming. Still, when she heard the light tap on the front door, the serving spoon fell from her hand.

"Great," she muttered. "Show him what a klutz you are." She put the spoon in the sink and rushed to the door.

She took a big breath and forced herself to peep out the viewer, just in case, and exhaled. Then, smile in place, she let Darien in.

"Hi, baby." He touched his mouth to hers briefly. "I hope I didn't take too long."

"No." Brooke closed the door. "Everything's still warm." He stood in the doorway and just stared at her instead of moving farther into the apartment.

"Everything?"

"Yeah." Brooke nodded. Then she noticed the heat in his gaze and her eyes widened. "Oh."

"Yeah, 'oh.'" He grinned.

"Are you..." She stopped and cleared her throat. "Are you ready for dinner?"

"I'm ready for anything you have for me."

"Darien. Stop that."

"Baby, we haven't even gotten started yet." He chuckled and Brooke swore she saw a dimple in his left cheek.

"Are we going to eat dinner?"

"Okay, I'll cool it." He cleared his throat. "Yes, we are going to eat the delicious meal you prepared. Lead the way." He grinned again.

They sat, and Brooke gave thanks. Then she smiled at him. "When I asked the Lord to bless the hands that prepared the food, I was including Ida, without whom this meal would not be possible."

"Oh, yeah?"

115

"Yeah. I didn't try to compete with her expertise." She passed him the collards.

"You didn't fix this with your own two little hands?"

"Depends on what you mean by 'fixed.' I warmed them up." They laughed.

The conversation was light and relaxed as they ate. Their relationship had turned another corner. Darien insisted on helping clean the kitchen, and Brooke couldn't stop from feeling it was natural for them to work together like this. If God willed it, they would have many more opportunities.

When they finished, Brooke put on music, and they sat on the couch sharing bits and pieces of their lives before they met and getting to know each other better.

"Guess it's time for me to go. I don't want to wear out my welcome," Darien said at eleven as he stood. "Besides, we're both on duty tomorrow morning."

They walked to the door and kissed goodnight. Darien left after pointing out they were having dinner at his place the next day. Brooke smiled as she locked up.

The world and its problems and dangers were far from them. If the Lord was willing, it would stay there. If not, He would give them strength to handle whatever came their way.

The next day the media was full of information about the arrest of Manuel Lomita. Brooke learned more than she wanted to know about the drug lord. *Terrorism comes in different flavors,* she thought as the story of his escapades on both sides of the border came to light. *Chalk one up for our side.*

Darien called to tell her his shift changed. An emergency arose, and he and his partner were moved to second shift until further notice.

Brooke missed him already. She wished she could discuss the news with Darien. She wished she could discuss anything with him. Or nothing. She just wanted to be with him.

THREE DAYS LATER, Darien arrived home at midnight. He missed Brooke. He had wrestled with his situation since they were last together and came to a decision. He loved her and wanted her in his life forever. The idea of marrying her seemed right. He was tempted to call her, but he didn't want to interrupt her rest. She needed to be alert for duty in the morning. He smiled. No need to rush. He was tempted to buy a ring as soon as the shops opened, but thought better of it. He didn't want to purchase something she didn't like. After all, he intended for her to wear it for the rest of her life. Too bad he couldn't make time fly until they were both off. He shook his head as he unlocked his door. This love thing was something else.

CHAPTER FIFTEEN

"WE MUST DO something quickly." Desano Velez spoke in a whisper, but his voice was harsh enough to carry as much weight as a shout. His glare at the five others crowded into the shack added to the heaviness. They shifted on the packing crates that served as chairs. "I tell you, I am not going to let them keep Manuel. I cannot forget all we've been to each other. We are *compadres* for many, many years." Desano stood. The table creaked when he pounded it with each of his next words and the thick stump of a candle in the middle flickered. "I will not leave *mi amigo* in their prison like that. I will not leave him to die, and do nothing to get him out. A patrol officer was killed. I know that. I do not care. Maybe he is the one who did this. Even if he is not, he was there. What do you think they will do to Manuel? He is not even *Americano*. The gringos, they put many of their own to death, especially in Texas. What you think they will do to him?" His voice rose to a shout, but he didn't care. The next house was a mile away. He didn't wait for an answer. "Manuel, him and me, we go way back."

118

"We know," Carlito said. "You have said this thing to us many times."

Desano continued as if he hadn't been interrupted. "He is like *mi hermano*, my brother, you know? We were *niños*, little children, together in the village. His *mamacita*, she is like a second mama to me." Desano paced the floor of the cabin. Carlito coughed at the dust Desano stirred up. The gazes of the five sitting at the table followed his movement.

"That is the chance he took," Leonardo pointed out for the third time. "Manuel, he should not have gone up there. He went before to make sure everything was the way he wanted it." He glared at Desano. "You know that—you went with him two times. You seen for yourself how we took territory one corner at a time. We made the Crips back off—the mighty Crips. Ha!" He laughed. "That is huge. Things were just about set. We even had a little *dinero* coming in. Manuel, he knew the *Americanos* were looking for him. He should have trusted Tonio to finish setting things up so our *compadres* could increase distribution when they got the new supplies."

"Manuel did not get where he is by trusting nobody."

"*Si*. You got that right," Leonardo said. "He was caught because he *did not* trust nobody, not even his *primos*, his cousins, not his *amigos*. He did not tell us what he had in mind—that he would go up there without one of us, without one of his *compadres* who knew how to handle things. If he was going again, why did he take two green *niños* and not one of us? He knew they do not know how to do nothing." Leonardo's face tightened. "He did not even tell you, did he? If he did, you woulda been with him and your *mamacita* would be weeping about you right now. Maybe you two were not as close as you think. Maybe *you* are the only one who thinks you are like brothers."

"What do you say? What you mean by that?" Desano rushed at Leonardo. "You are saying Manuel...he did not trust me?" The two men stood chest to chest. If either took a deep breath, he would have bumped the other.

"Stop." Esteban jumped up and shoved them apart. "We will not do Manuel no good if we fight each other. We must decide what we are going to do."

"What we will *not* do is leave Manual in prison and do nothing." Desano folded his arms across his chest.

"And what we will *not* do is go to the jail and try to get him out. Then we would all be where he is now, and how would that help Manuel? Huh, *mi amigo*?" Leonardo backed up a step and Desano did the same. "Besides, we do not even know where they keep him."

"We can find out."

"How you do think we can do that?"

"I do not know yet, but we will think of something."

"We should talk with our partners. Perhaps they will have an idea." Carlito looked hopeful.

"We will not talk to them. What do you think they will do?" Desano spun around to face Carlito. "They blow up themselves. They do not care for nobody else, neither. I have seen the news. Almost every day, some of them in their country drive into a group of people and blow themselves into more pieces than you think possible. Their mamas come on television. They cry, but they say they are glad their sons die for the cause."

He glared at Carlito, then at the others. "Do you think our partners care that Manuel is sitting in some prison? Do you think they want him free?" He started pacing again. "I was against having anything to do with them, anyway. I tell Manuel that. That group, they frighten me. It is not natural to not care about dying. It is not normal to do something you know will get you killed, and that is the end of the subject."

"We were *all* against it when they came to us," Leonardo pointed out. "All except Manuel. But he would not listen. He did not listen to *you*. He decided to join up with them like he made the decision that got him where he is right now. He did not need to go to Houston again. His cousins, they know what to do. Everything was ready. They hold territory like we planned. They got rid of the ones in our way. We got a little good money coming through already and more on the way. Manuel, he had no reason to go up there himself. No reason." Leonardo turned and pointed at Desano. "Now you want us to try to get him out of the trouble he got his own self into."

"I know we didn't need the others," Desano admitted. "It would have taken longer, but we could have got the supply and moved it ourselves. We did not need no outsiders. No strangers. Especially strangers like that." He shook his head. "You know I tried to talk Manuel out of it. You heard me tell him we could do this on our own, but he was in a hurry. He wanted the money now." He shook his head. "He was like that when we were young. Get an idea and go with it right away without thinking it through." Desano looked at the others. His steady gaze rested on each for a few seconds before moving on. "Still, that is not a reason to forget him."

"There is no way we can get him out even if we agree."

"We can come up with a plan," Sonia said. She stood and walked to the center of the room, then turned to face them. "Soon they will move him and put him farther away and in a tighter place. We must do something first."

"What you think our partners will do when they find out the *Americanos* have Manuel? Manuel, he knows much about them.

What do you think they would do if they know about him?" Estaban asked the question that was in the back of Desano's mind. He saw how anybody in the partners' way was dealt with. He never witnessed them do anything, but the results spoke volumes and he knew whose work it was. Bombs weren't the only thing that group knew about.

"The one thing they will not do is worry about getting him out," Estaban said. "Manuel, he knows more about them than the rest of us do," he repeated. "He could cut a deal. *Americanos* got lots of interest in those crazies who don't mind dying. Why don't we wait and let Manuel make a deal?"

"The *Americanos* will not let him go even if he could guarantee they get all who are in charge in that desert over there *and* down here. A patrol agent got killed, and Manuel was there."

"Whatever we decide, I think we need to move out of here," Sonia said. "Our partners will not be happy that somebody who knows as much as Manuel is in the *Americano* jail. They kill themselves. They will have no problem killing Manuel and us too." Sonia's face contorted with the weight of her statement. "We all know too much."

"It is time to move on anyway." Desano spoke up. "But we are not finished with this thing about Manuel."

"No, we are not," Sonia added.

"First we must come up with a plan."

"I have an idea," Sonia said. "We don't need much time because it is simple."

"We must leave here now." Desano looked toward the door. "I am surprised the *locos* are not here already. I know they have seen the news. They probably know more than the reporters do. They have their own way of finding out things."

"I can tell you what I have in mind as we move," Sonia said.

"*Bueno*. That is good because we will not stay here any longer. It is not safe."

Desano sent Estaban to notify their contacts along the pipeline to wait until he contacted them again. The rest gathered the few things they had, then left. They didn't slip out one by one, not this time. They would go to the place they had before they joined the others. They wouldn't come back to this place, so it didn't matter if they were seen. Besides, they didn't have much time.

The good thing about having so few in the group was that it wouldn't take long for them to set up again. The bad thing was that Manuel wasn't with them. If Sonia's plan worked, though, that wouldn't be for long.

CHAPTER SIXTEEN

"I'M GOING TO let you drive today, Alonzo," Brooke said to her partner. "But you better follow my instructions, or I swear, you'll still be riding shotgun when you retire. You got that?" she asked as they got into her car.

He saluted her. "I got that, boss."

"I mean it, Alonzo. You better not make me regret this," she added as she buckled her seatbelt.

"I won't. I promise." Alonzo held up his right hand, then fastened his seatbelt and started the car. "By the book. That's how I'll play it. By the book."

"If you *do* start to drive regularly, you're gonna have to use your car. The patrol hasn't replaced all of the vehicles destroyed by the bombs."

"Yeah. I know." He pulled from the lot.

"Your lady can do without a car for the day?"

"My lady is cool. She can plan her day around my schedule."

"Okay. Just don't—"

"I know, I know. Don't mess up. I hear you loud and clear." He looked at her after he turned onto Elizabeth Street. "Don't worry, I won't make you sorry."

They passed cars streaming in from Mexico by way of the restored International Bridge. They waited for the light to change, then rode toward Route 281, their assigned area. Soon they left the town behind. Buildings gave way to farm fences.

Alonzo talked as he drove, but Brooke's attention centered on the surroundings. This isolated area was a known entry for those without papers. The chain link fence would do nothing to keep anybody out who wanted in. It would do little to even slow them down.

"We have to pay attention in this area," Brooke said.

"Yeah. I remember what you said the other day," Alonzo responded when she mentioned it. "This is where farmers complain about damages to their fences." He glanced at the Rio Grande in the distance to the left. "Think this is one of the places where they're gonna put up a wall when they build them? It's kind of isolated and the fence don't look so good."

"It's probably part of the plans."

"Maybe they'll use one of those electronic fences. That would be cool. Hey. Look. There. Up ahead." Alonzo pointed toward a man standing beside the road about a quarter of a mile ahead. He frantically waved his hands. The front door as well as the back door of his old car was open. "What do you think that's about?" Alonzo asked.

"I don't know. I'll call it in." Brooke glanced at the thick brush on both sides of the road and frowned. "I don't like this."

"I don't know. Don't look like nothing much to me." Alonzo slowed the car. "His vehicle probably broke down, and he needs to call somebody for help. Bet he doesn't have a cell phone. He doesn't

125

look like he can afford one. He needs to call a tow truck or something."

"Follow procedure, Alonzo." Brooke spoke slowly, as if she were talking to a preschooler. "Call it in and we wait. This doesn't feel right. Do not drive any closer to the car. We wait for directions from headquarters."

"Okay, okay. I hear you." He continued to stare at the car. "But we don't know why he's stopped," he said as he pulled a short distance behind the car and parked. "It might be something we can handle ourselves. No sense wasting a trip for another team if it's something we can take care of. If the driver was doing something wrong, he wouldn't be trying to attract attention, would he? I think we should just check it out." He opened the door.

"Alonzo Keating," Brooke yelled as he left the vehicle and started walking toward the other car. "You come back here. We will follow procedure on this."

When Alonzo ignored her, Brooke quickly called in their location and filled the dispatcher in about the situation. Then, fussing at Alonzo as if he could hear her, she scrambled out. Hand on her gun, she ran toward the car.

"*Mi esposa*," the man waving his hands said to Alonzo. He pointed to the car. "*Por favor*. Please to help her, *por favor*. The *bebe*, he is coming. Please, *señor*. You help us?"

Alonzo, his hand resting on his holstered gun, watched as a very pregnant woman struggled from the back seat of the car. Once she stood in the road, she grasped her middle, moaned, and doubled over.

"She's ready to deliver?" Alonzo asked in Spanish as he stopped within a few feet of the man. "It's time for the baby? It's coming now?" He took his hand off his weapon and, hand outstretched to the woman, hurried toward her.

126

"*Si*," the man answered. His eyes followed Alonzo, and he glanced quickly at the brush to the side of the road, then to the man behind the wheel. Then many things happened at once.

A shot came from the man standing. A second came from the woman as she let go of her stomach and pulled a gun from her pocket. More gunfire erupted from the bushes, and Alonzo collapsed into the road.

At the first shot, Brooke dropped to the dirt and got off some shots. Her first hit the man in the chest, and he fell to the ground. Her second hit the woman, who cried out and dropped her gun. She held her hand over her shoulder and scampered back into the car.

Next, Brooke returned the fire coming from the brush as she scrambled toward the cover of their car, because it was closer. She could deal with the occupants later. Right now, the bigger threat was those hidden.

Answering fire from the bushes told her either there was more than one shooter, or she wasn't as good a shot as her records at the academy indicated.

She crawled toward the safety of the assailants' car, praying the shooters were only on the one side of the road.

A bullet from the brush sped a string of pain down her arm just before she reached the car. *Keep going.* She resisted the urge to cover the wound with her other hand and instead rolled onto her side and fired again into the brush. An answering cry rang out from that area. Good.

The rear wheel of the car provided her cover. She reached toward Alonzo, where he lay still with a slow ooze of blood coming from his body. The last thing she was aware of was a blow to her head.

CHAPTER SEVENTEEN

AFTER THE FIRST half of their shift, where the most exciting thing to happen was the odometer turning to three zeroes at the end, Darien suggested to Jack they stop for an early lunch. This was one time he was glad for Jack's going along with every suggestion. He knew it was irrational to expect an early lunch to make the shift go faster, but he'd deal with finding a way to speed up the second part later. He missed Brooke.

It felt as if months had passed since he held her. He was anxious to see her face when he proposed. He'd get down on one knee. Follow the whole tradition. He grinned. She'd say yes. She had to. She loved him as much as he loved her. She couldn't love him more. That wasn't possible. He released a long, slow breath. *Patience, Darien.* He struggled to concentrate on their surroundings as he drove to the place he had in mind for today's lunch.

He parked in the lot of a restaurant he and Brooke hadn't visited yet. That's why he picked it. He didn't need added distraction. He was having enough trouble trying to keep her off his mind.

He went to a table close to the wall and sat facing the door.

"*Hola*, officers," the waitress said as she came over to Darien's table with the coffee pot and two heavy mugs. "What'll it be?"

Darien and Jack gave their orders and received their food before they finished the first cup of coffee.

They were halfway through their sandwiches when two men in animated conversation entered and stopped abruptly when they spotted Darien and Jack. They glanced at each other. They seemed to be arguing, but glanced frequently in their direction.

Darien went on full-alert. An agent never knew who they'd run up against when in uniform. There was no way of knowing what was on a stranger's agenda until they let them know. Sometimes that happened too late.

He eased his hand onto his gun and unfastened the holster strap, though the gun at his side remained hidden by the red and white-checked tablecloth. His stare stayed on the two men as they approached.

"We are so sorry about what happened, *mis amigos*," one man said glancing, from Darien to Jack and back to Darien. "My name is Miguel Perez. This is my friend, Gomez. I own the little hotel on Fourteenth Street. The patrol gives good protection to us business owners. I, myself, have called on your good graces several times and you have helped me."

"What happened? What are you talking about?" Darien asked. He sat up straighter.

"The shooting. It happened a little while ago."

"Shooting? What shooting?" He jumped up, causing his chair to tumble backward. "What happened?"

"You have not heard? They have not told you? I hate to be the one to give you such bad news about your fellow patrol officers."

"What happened? Where?"

"The shooting was over on Route 281, the Military Highway. An announcer just told it on the radio. She broke into my favorite song to tell about an incident."

"What did they say?"

"They did not say so much. An officer was shot and an ambulance was on the way to the scene. They say they will tell us more when they find out more."

"I will bet every news program has somebody going out there too," Gomez said. "You know how reporters sometimes get to the scene before the police. It is almost as if they know ahead of time when and where something is gonna happen."

"My sister, Marta, works in a news room, Gomez," Miguel said. "The news people do not got nothin' to do with what happens. People nearby who see something will call the station, and the news people, they send out a team to investigate. The news people, they are supposed to report the news to the public. That is what they do. It is their job. If they did not tell us, we would never know nothin'."

"I did not say they got anything to do with what happens," Gomez said. "I just said they get there so fast it is as if—"

"Where did it happen?" Darien grabbed Miguel's arms. "Exactly where on Route 281?"

"I...I..." He swallowed hard. "They said something about near Service Road 3248."

"3248. You sure about that?"

"Si. Yeah." His head bobbed up and down quickly. "I...I am sure. I got a cousin who lives close to that road. He has a farm nearby. The patrol, they give him protection from those who do not belong here when they come onto his land and do damage." He tried to shrug, but Darien's hold prevented the movement. "You are hurting my arms, Officer."

"Sorry." Darien let go of the man and turned to Jack. "Let's go. We're heading out there." He threw more than enough money onto the table.

"We're going there? Now?" Jack asked as he looked up at Darien from his seat. "But...but, sir, that's not our area. Shouldn't we wait until we get orders? I...I can't afford to get in trouble. I'm...I'm still on probation. I don't want to have to go back to the academy and go through all that training again. It was rough enough the first time. I don't want to have to—"

"I'm the senior officer, and I say we go. Any repercussions will be on me since I gave the order, and protocol says you follow my orders. I'll make sure you're in the clear." Darien glared and Jack scrambled to his feet. "Bring the rest of your sandwich if you want to. You can finish it in the car."

"But I thought we weren't supposed to eat in a moving vehicle while we're on patrol. I don't want to—"

Darien reached across Jack, grabbed the sandwich, wrapped it in a napkin, and thrust it at him. "Take this and let's go."

He was at the door before he finished his sentence. He didn't look back. If Jack intended to ride with him, the green officer had better be close behind. If he wasn't there, Darien would leave him.

Jack was still trying to buckle his seatbelt when Darien placed the light on top of the car and flipped the switch. Then, tires squealing, he left the lot and tore down the street.

When he reached the end of their assigned area, Darien didn't even slow. Instead, he sped toward the intersection the man in the restaurant mentioned. Darien pictured the area. It was an isolated crossroad miles into Brooke's assigned area.

He knew the location well. He and Brooke drove it several times when she was helping him get oriented with the sector. It wasn't far from a small village, but you wouldn't know it once you left the last street. Very few places around Brownsville were more isolated than that spot.

His hold tightened on the steering wheel as, against his will, the picture of that section stayed in his mind.

Thick bushes grew on both sides. In many places, they were taller than a person. The closest farm was across the *Resaca de la Palma*, a stream which flowed from the main reservoir toward the west.

In dry season, the area looked like fertile land that nobody wanted to use, but when Brownsville received the usual rainfall, the area resembled a lake. Often during the rainy season, the road flooded, and the usual sparse traffic had to detour miles around it. They hadn't had enough rain for years to make that happen, but the brush continued to grow.

You'd better be okay, Brooke, Darien thought as the side streets he passed blurred. *Please let her be all right.*

He pushed the accelerator harder. He didn't realize his car could go so fast. He wished it had even more power.

An ambulance screamed past them, headed for town, and Darien paused for a second, torn.

Should he follow it? What if Brooke was inside? He frowned. But what if she wasn't? What if she was at the scene ahead giving her report? He was closer to the area the men mentioned than he was to town. He accelerated even faster than before.

Ten miles farther, still several hundred yards from the intersection, Darien slowed, but he knew they had reached the scene of the incident.

At first glance, because of all of the activity, it looked as if a country fair might be ahead. A closer look showed an ambulance in the center and an emergency team near it.

Patrol cars, as well as what must've been a few agents' personal vehicles on the scene, were scattered on the fringes of the activity. Vans and cars bearing logos of the local news media were outside of the crime scene perimeter.

Yellow caution tape hung across the road and wrapped around anything capable of holding it. News cameras pointed at the area and each had a person standing in front, talking. It sounded to Darien as if a thousand conversations were going on at the same time but not a word separated from the others. Darien didn't care. He didn't want to hear anything from them. Anything they said would be speculation, and he wanted facts. He needed to know if he was worried for nothing.

"Call in our location," Darien told Jack as he stopped the car. He jumped out and ran toward the tape, leaving Jack to turn off the engine. He ducked under the tape and rushed to an officer he knew.

"What happened, Roy?" he asked as he grabbed a man's arm and seized his attention from the conversation he was having with another officer.

"Not sure yet, Darien. We've got one officer down and one missing. We believe we have an assailant also hit."

"Who's involved? What officer? What do you mean down?" He didn't want to ask if down meant dead in this case.

"I mean shot. He's on his way to the hospital. He's in pretty bad shape. The ambulance probably passed you on your way here."

"He? It's a male officer shot? What's his name?"

"Alonzo Keating."

Darien's heart squeezed and at the same time, he felt as if he took a blow to the stomach. For a few seconds, his brain refused to function. "Where's his partner? Where's Brooke?"

"We don't know."

"What do you mean, you don't know? They're partners. They were on duty together."

"We know. We're looking for her now." He pointed to the area on both sides of the road. Darien noticed people scattered in the brush, walking slowly through the thick growth.

"If she was anywhere near, she'd come out," Darien said. "As much noise as is going on here, she couldn't miss it." He stared at Roy. Roy just gazed silently back. Darien gasped. "If she could. What aren't you telling me?"

"We found evidence she might be wounded."

"Wounded? What evidence?"

"We found blood too far away from Officer Keating to be his. It was away from the slain assailant too."

"Blood? How much? A lot? Where?"

"Over there." Roy pointed to a small clearing in the road. "Not so much that she couldn't have moved to cover. We have the second ambulance standing by in case."

"What happened?"

"From what we know, a car was stopped at the side of the road, and agents Hudson and Keating stopped to investigate."

"Brooke knows better than that. She would follow protocol. She wouldn't rush into a situation like that. She'd call it in and wait as per procedure."

"She did call it in. That's how we know about the car, and how we were able to get here so fast. If we hadn't, I don't think the ambulance carrying Officer Keating to the hospital would have needed the siren." He stared at Darien. "If she's in this area, we'll find her."

"I'm helping."

"Did the commander approve your being here?" Darien's answer was a hard stare. Roy hesitated a few seconds. "Report to Agent Hopkins. He's in charge of the operation." Roy pointed to an officer who was giving directions. "He'll tell you where you can help the most."

In a few minutes, Darien was at the far end of the search area. He started inside the fence around the ranch, searched the area along it quickly but thoroughly, and then began working his way out to the scene.

Jack walked a few feet to the left doing the same. Civilians had come to help in the search. Enough people joined the hunt to examine every foot of ground they explored.

At one point somebody shouted. Darien's hopes lifted, but they plunged when it turned out to be a small patch of old blood. He almost wished it were Brooke's. If it was, she might be nearby.

Darien heard the officer in charge assign personnel to visit every farm and house within a five mile radius. He watched them leave, then continued to search his area. When they all returned, he went to hear the reports.

The agents received permission from the owners, and the houses and outbuildings were investigated. They didn't find any sign of Brooke.

Darien finally returned to the place from which he started. He was the last to stop searching. Some of the vehicles were gone.

When the last media vehicle pulled away, Darien stared at it until it disappeared on the horizon. He had to accept as fact Brooke wasn't in the area. As thoroughly as they had searched, they would have found a safety pin if one had been in the weeds. He stood staring at the spot of blood on the road, the one believed to belong to her. Then he slowly looked around as if Brooke would miraculously appear.

Where was she? If the people in the car she reported had her, what was their reason for kidnapping a patrol officer? Where did they take her? How badly was she hurt?

Darien glanced at the fence dividing the two countries. *No.* He shook his head. They wouldn't try to take her into Mexico. Crossing the border would be too risky and what purpose would it serve? No, they wouldn't, he thought again. But he kept staring at the fence.

CHAPTER EIGHTEEN

"WE DID, IT, amigo. We did it." Estaban leaned forward from the back seat and patted Desano on the shoulder. "No problem. As the gringos say, 'piece of cake.'"

"I told you. You got to learn to put your trust in me." Desano glanced over his shoulder at his friend and then farther back to the bridge they rapidly left behind. He returned his attention to the road in front of them.

"We did have a problem." In the passenger seat, Leonardo turned to face Estaban and leaned close to him. Estaban angled away. "How do you forget Carlito so quickly?" Leonardo's words filled the car. "The gringa agent, she kill him and you say 'no problem.' We could not even bring him back with us for fear we would be stopped at the border because *she* takes up too much space."

"I am sorry about Carlito," Estaban said. He leaned against the door. "He was my friend as well, but he knew the danger we faced. He wanted to free Manuel too."

"He did not think he would be killed." Leonardo spat out each word.

"We did not think so, neither. But it is done," Desano interrupted. "We cannot undo it. None of us thought we would lose one of our own, but it happened. It could happen any time in the business we are in. We all knew that before we started. We agreed it was worth the money to take a chance. What happened to Carlito is part of the job description." Desano glanced at Leonardo. "Besides, we killed one of theirs too."

Leonardo turned his attention to the scene outside the window. He shifted in his seat.

"You okay, Sonia?" Desano asked the woman sitting beside him. She no longer clutched her now flat stomach. Instead, she held her fingers over the piece of shirt Desano tied around her upper arm. "Sorry we had to be so rough when we got you into the car."

"I understand. I too am sorry about Carlito. His *mamacita* will be heartbroken." She glanced at Leonardo, then back to Desano. "My arm, it is nothing. It hurts, but the bullet went through. I will be all right. I am sorry we cannot say the same about Carlito." Her words stopped for a while. She sat up straighter. "As for my arm, it was worth it. It was worth more than this. Soon Manuel will be back with us."

"*Si.*" Desano nodded. "Soon." He glanced toward the floor in back. "For now, we get her out of there soon. We need her alive."

He drove for another fifteen minutes before he turned down a side road. They were about thirty miles into Mexico, but the *Americanos* had a long reach. Their money would buy a lot of information.

Desano looked at the road ahead to make sure nothing was coming. Then he examined the open land on both sides. Nobody was in sight. Still, he drove several more miles before he pulled the car to the side. A small house sat in the distance across a field of brown grass. Desano stared at it for a minute. He didn't see anyone. "*Bueno.*" He nodded and smiled. "Good."

He left the driver's seat. Estaban and Leonardo hurried from the rear of the car. After satisfying themselves again that no traffic approached from either direction, and no people were in view, the men went to work.

Quickly they lifted the false floor in the back. Daylight flooded over the agent lying on her side in the shallow hollow, but she didn't move. She didn't even blink.

"She is all right, *si*? She is not dead, is she?" Desano asked. "We need her alive for our plan to work. They will want proof she is with us."

Estaban leaned closer and glared down at her. Then he poked her shoulder. "She is still with us," he said as she winced from his touch. "But Leonardo, he hit her hard."

"We had to be sure she would not wake before we left her country," Leonardo answered. "I do not desire to be caught holding a U.S. Border Patrol Agent prisoner. If we get busted with her, we will be locked away with Manuel or worse. Maybe no one would hear from us ever again."

"We are lucky all their care at the bridges is about people going *into* their country and they do not care about those coming into ours." Desano laughed. "They do not even bother to stop cars anymore. Our agents don't bother with food and clothes coming in, either. It is so easy, now, to come home."

"We lost Carlito, but it was a good plan," Estaban said as he nodded. "I was not sure it would succeed, but it worked."

"It has worked so far, but we will not have a fiesta yet. We still do not have Manuel with us," Desano pointed out.

"We will," Sonia said. "The Americans will gladly trade him for one of their own. They do not want responsibility for the death of one of their agents. Many were lost the day with the bombs. My Manuel will be with me soon. I know it."

"I hope you are right," Leonardo said.

"Bind the wound on her arm," Desano ordered as he pointed down at their prisoner. "We do not need her to die because we did not take care of her wound. A dead agent is of no use. They are sure to demand proof she is alive before they make the trade."

They pulled her from the hollow and laid her on the back floor. Estaban tugged at her sleeve. "I cannot get to the wound."

"Cut the sleeve off."

Estaban took out his pocket knife and did so. Then he tried to pull the sleeve free. "It is no use. It will not come free. It is stuck with her blood."

"Move out of the way." Desano shoved Estaban aside. "I must do everything. Give me the bottle of water," he said to Sonia.

He grabbed it and poured enough water over the spot to soak it. Then he waited. After a minute, he pulled hard. The woman cried out as the sleeve came loose, but she didn't open her eyes. The wound began to bleed again, covering old blood with new. Desano discarded the sleeve out the window. "Give me your shirt," he ordered Leonardo.

"What do you want with my shirt?" Leonardo asked. Still, he took it off. "Hey. What are you doing?" He yelled as Desano ripped a piece from the bottom. "That shirt is my favorite. My *mamacita* gave it to me. Why you not use somebody else's shirt? Why not your own?"

"When our next deal goes through, and big money starts coming back to us, you can buy a hundred shirts. You can give your *mamacita* enough money to buy whatever she wants. Our village

140

will have all the food they need, and the children will no longer look at us with hungry eyes. We will have more money than we can spend. So do not talk about an old shirt!"

He wrapped the strip of cloth around the fresh blood that had started a new path down the woman's arm. She groaned as he tied the knot over the wound and patted it. Then he put her back into the hollow.

When he let her go, she moved just enough to bring her knees to her chest, but she still never opened her eyes. Instead, she remained huddled in the small space.

They put the covering back in place and loaded into the car. Desano quickly drove away.

He continued to drive deeper into the countryside, speeding along the isolated road despite its high bumps and deep ruts. They had not reached safety yet. They were still too close to the border and didn't have much time. He would not stop until they arrived at their headquarters many miles away.

The American government would bring pressure on the Mexican government when those searching did not find a second body. They would know an agent was taken, but they would not know where. How long before they concluded she'd been brought across the border? How long before the Mexican government would help the *Americanos* search?

Desano and his group had to reach their headquarters before any of that happened. They had to free Manuel or all of this would be for nothing.

An hour later the woman mumbled. Desano pulled over and they quickly opened the floor again.

She mumbled again, asking for water in English and Spanish. Estaban lifted her head, and she gulped down half a bottle without stopping, then she was quiet. Through it all, she never opened her eyes. They quickly put the flooring back in place and hurried back into the car.

After another hour, Desano drove onto an even narrower road. He moved slowly over the ruts. Still, the undercarriage bumped the middle more than once and the car brushed against weeds growing thick along the sides.

Little daylight was left as they turned yet again. It would take a big stretch of imagination to call this road they were driving on anything but a footpath.

Finally, after following the many turns that took them out of sight of the road and deeper into the underbrush, Desano stopped outside a small shack nestled against an area thick with scruffy weeds growing down an embankment.

"Hurry and get her inside," Desano ordered. Leonardo and Estaban hauled her to her feet. They ignored her groans in response to their rough treatment.

"Where am I?" she whispered as they dragged her from the car. "My head." She tried to touch the injury, but they held her arms. "That hurts," she protested.

"She is bleeding," Estaban said and moved his hand from Brooke's arm.

"Put her over there," Desano said as he pointed to the cot against the back wall.

They half-walked and half-dragged her. "Sonia, see if she has identification papers. We must tell them which of their agents we have."

Sonia rummaged through the prisoner's pockets.

"Here." Sonia smiled as she held up the identification papers.

"I will take that." Desano reached for it, flipped it open, and read. "Brooke Hudson." He looked her way. "Welcome, Agent

Brooke Hudson. I hope you enjoy our accommodations." He laughed.

"Now what?" Leonardo asked, grabbing Desano's attention.

"Now I go back across the border. Tomorrow. I will write a note telling them that we have one of their own, Agent Brooke Hudson, and we want Manuel in trade. Then I will give some child a little money to take it to an agent."

"What if you get caught?"

"When will you learn to trust me? Look at what we did by following my plan. We grabbed a Border Patrol Agent and got her across the border with little problem. I am not forgetting Carlito," he added when Leonardo opened his mouth. "Getting her here, that was the hard part. The next part of our plan will be easy."

"How you know the *niño* will take the note to an agent? How do you know he will not just take the money you give him and keep going?"

"I will promise him more money when he returns to me after he delivers it."

"But he will bring agents with him. What are we to do with her if you do not return?" Leonardo pointed at the agent.

"*Stupido.* I will not be there." He shook his head. "I do not see why Manuel thought you would make a good *compadre*."

"I am not stupid. Sometimes you do things and do not think them through to the end. You are just like Manuel in that."

"Do not talk about Manuel." Desano walked close to Leonardo. "If not for him we would still be trying to sneak north to do hard work for some *gringo* who would pay us little money. Instead, we will have more money than we ever thought possible, and we will not have to dig in the dirt or work in the hot sun. Manuel is the one who thought of our business. He got it started. He helped us seize our own territory across the border."

"He also tied us to those others," Leonardo reminded Desano. "I do not want to think what they will do when they learn Manuel is in the American prison."

"Then do not think of it. They do not know of this place." Desano looked at Estaban. "Go outside and make a fire. We have worked hard today, and I am hungry." He looked at the others. "Tonight we will eat beans and rice. Tomorrow I will take the note. I will stop for food and bring it back to you, if I can. If I cannot, we will eat beans and rice again. It will not be for much longer."

"What will you do after you send the note?"

"I will think of a way to have them contact us. They will not risk harm coming to their agent. Do not worry. We will make the trade here in Mexico. It will go well. Soon we will have Manuel back with us, and our people will start to bring our money to us. As hungry as the *Americanos* are for what we sell, it will not take long for us to get paid. All we must do now is wait. My plan will succeed." He glared at Leonardo. "Be patient and do not worry."

"Why do you not use the telephone to call them after you get over to their side of the border?" Estaban asked. "That would be safer than a note."

"They can find where you are if you use a phone. Don't you know anything?"

"They can only find you if you are on the phone a long time," Sonia said. "If you have it worked out in your head, and tell them quickly, it will work. That way is better than to give a note to a *niño*. No?"

Desano was silent for many minutes. "Perhaps that way will work better." His words were low. "I will tell them to let Manuel cross the bridge on International Boulevard on Saturday evening. He will blend in with the many people coming back home. Manuel will know to come here when we are not at the other place. I will tell them we will release their agent when we hear from Manuel."

"Do you think they will believe you?"

"I will say we have no reason to keep her."

"Will we let her go?"

"Why should we not? She will be of no further use to us, and we can travel faster without her."

"But she will know our faces. She will know this place."

"It does not matter that she sees us. She will not see us again. They will not find us. Mexico is a big country."

"We will keep her until Manuel comes here?" Sonia asked.

"*Si.*"

"That is a long time."

"Do you have something better to do?"

"No."

"When Manuel gets here we will let her go right here. She will get home on her own. She will be walking. By the time she has reached someone, we will be somewhere else. It does not matter where."

"What of the others? Our *loco* partners? What if they get to Manuel first?"

"They will not have time. Manuel will be on his way back before they can do anything, before they even know the *Americanos* have him."

"If Manuel decides to work with those people again, I will not stay. I will go home," Leonardo said. "It is better to live and work hard than to die with a lot of money."

"I do not think he will take partners again," Desano said. He turned their attention from their prisoner and back to their business.

145

CHAPTER NINETEEN

BROOKE WAS AWAKE, but kept her eyes closed. Their plan to let her go did not ease her mind. The Customs Border Patrol, like all other American government departments, did not negotiate for the release of prisoners under any circumstances. She was on her own.

"Where am I?" Brooke mumbled and shifted on the cot as if just regaining consciousness. They didn't need to know she heard their plans. As soon as she got a chance, she'd do what she could to stop them.

When she sat, she grabbed her head and bent over. Pain shot from the back of her skull forward, worse than after the bombing. It hurt as if somebody was using a sledge hammer to pound on her head. The pain seemed to pierce her eyes. Still, she forced them open and looked around. She needed to know as much as she could as soon as she could.

Dirt shed from the adobe walls lay in piles on the floor around the perimeter. Her cot and several others were the only furniture except for a roughhewn table in the middle of the small room. Five packing crates surrounded it as mock chairs. Several more wooden boxes sat in a corner. Another was beside her cot and one more was beside the door.

A fireplace that looked as if it would fall apart if anybody sneezed was built into a side wall. A door was across from the fireplace. It was windowless, but there was a dirty window beside it. Another window was above her bed. She didn't have to worry about daylight coming in and making her headache worse. That window, as well as the others, looked as if it'd never been washed. Another window was on the wall opposite her bed.

Weak light managed to filter through the dirt on the glass and tell her that it was still daytime.

"So you are awake." A man with cold eyes glared down at her.

"May I have some water, please?" Brooke made her voice weaker than she felt.

Still holding her head with both hands, she slumped back against the wall. When she stopped moving, the pain eased to a tolerable ache, but the man didn't need to know that. Another ache, not as strong as the one in her head, throbbed in her arm when she moved it.

She heard some information from the conversation between the five people in the room, but she still had unanswered questions.

Where was she? Who had her? Drug smugglers? How many were there? Were these the only ones she had to be concerned about or were others nearby? And what were the circumstances regarding this Manuel they'd talked about?

She opened her eyes again, slowly this time. The door opened and three others came in. Brooke looked at the man who spoke to her. He must be the leader.

"Please. Water." Again she made her voice weak.

He turned and nodded to one of the others, who brought her a bottle. She didn't pretend thirst as she gulped the liquid. She wanted to ask questions, but knew she would get no answers. She'd learn as much as she could by listening. Now, more than at any other time, she was grateful the academy required all agents to be fluent in Spanish. She was also thankful she'd taken top honors in that class. Already she had learned things about these people from their conversations.

Were more people outside? She doubted it. The leader was the one who waved from beside the car when they stopped. The woman was the one pretending to be pregnant. Brooke noted her flat middle. It was a good plan. People were likely to stop for a woman who looked as if she was about to go into labor. Brooke frowned. *If it'd been up to me, I wouldn't have gone to the car. I would have waited for help as we were taught to do.* She thought of what'd happened. *Alonzo rushed to help, and he got killed for it. He found out the hard way why some rules are made.*

Brooke closed her eyes and said a prayer for him and his girlfriend. Then she said one for herself. She had to gain strength. She didn't know how much time she had, but she didn't think it was much. She prayed it would be enough.

Her captors ignored her, and she drifted off to sleep again.

When night came the kidnappers lit the candle on the table. They brought her a plate of beans and rice. The food was dry and flavorless, but she forced herself to eat. She would need her strength if she was to find a way out. No, that wasn't true. The Lord would help her. It wasn't *if* she found a way to escape, but *when* she found a way out. She looked at the food the others ate. Their meal was as sparse as hers.

As soon as her captors finished eating, they blew out the candle. The woman and one of the men settled onto cots. The others went outside. Brooke assumed they were to keep guard.

Were they close enough to the border to fear someone might come looking for her? She thought of Darien. If it could be done, he'd be the one. *Darien. Darien.* Despite the situation, she smiled. Then her smile faded quickly. For it to matter, she had to be alive. She had to do what she could to accomplish that.

She thanked God she was still breathing and asked Him to continue to be with her. As she prayed, she felt her stress ease. She drifted off to sleep.

Light slipping through the windows announced morning. Brooke opened her eyes to slits, but didn't move. She slowly turned her head, but only enough so she could see who was with her.

Two different kidnappers slept on the cots. They must've changed guards during the night. She had slept right through their moving about.

Breakfast was the same as dinner and just tasteless. Brooke ate every bean and every grain of rice.

As soon as they finished the meal, the leader—the one they called Desano—stood and faced the others.

"I am ready to leave. If I am not back in five days, and our people have come to start the trade, leave this place and go to our other one. We have not used it for a while, but it will be waiting. If our carriers have not come in that time, wait for them and tell them where we will be. It would be a shame to go through all the work to set up our operation and not have money coming back to us."

"If you are not back in five days' time and they have come, what do we do with her? Do we take her with us?" Leonardo nodded toward Brooke.

"If I do not come back in that time, it will mean they will not let Manuel go free. We will not need her. Kill her. Or set her free. Whatever you wish." He stared at Brooke. "But do not worry. I will be back."

"Why will it take so long?"

"We do not know if they have to bring him from far away. They may need time to decide. We will not fail to get Manuel free because I was not patient." He looked at the others. "Come outside. We will talk."

"What about her?" Sonia looked at Brooke.

"She is weak. And she is but one. What can she do against the five of us? Besides, she does not know where this place is. We do not need for someone to stay with her." He glanced at Brooke again.

Brooke forced herself to look away. She made herself continue to look weak. After a few seconds, Desano went outside, and the others followed.

Brooke could tell by the volume of their voices when they moved away from the door. She stood carefully. Her head still hurt, but she ignored it. When she climbed onto her cot and used her wounded arm for leverage, she grimaced. She prayed the cot would hold her weight. She thanked God when it did. She looked out the window.

The growth outside the window was mostly dry scrub brush, and there wasn't much of it. A few trees, standing far apart from each other, were living despite the dry conditions. The trees showed how steep the hill behind the shack was. Brooke considered the area for a few seconds. The trees would provide the only cover, and there were wide, low areas between them. Hills loomed in the distance, but they were too far away to give immediate cover. She had no idea where she was. Getting out was not her only problem, but she'd worry about the next step after she was free.

150

She ignored the throbbing protest from her wounded arm when she shoved at the window. It didn't budge. Of course it wouldn't be that easy. She explored around the wooden frame and didn't find any nails. Lack of use and dirt had to be the reasons why it wouldn't open. It certainly was not painted shut. This wood had never known such. Brooke hoped she had time to work on the window and that five days would be enough. Desano wouldn't be back before then. She shook her head slightly. If the Lord wanted it so, that would be enough time, and she'd have enough strength to do what was necessary. Her government wouldn't make a deal, and she didn't intend to be here for them to decide whether to let her live or die.

She heard the car drive off and assumed Desano left. She stepped down. She lay on the cot and waited, but the others stayed outside. Finally, she slipped over to the window beside the door and glanced out.

The bare area in front of the shack couldn't be considered a clearing any more than this building could be called a house. Tuffs of spindly grass grew here and there. Brush grew on both sides of the parking area.

Two beat-up cars crowded what little space there was. One car was without tires. Both vehicles looked as if they had been built from parts of other cars. She wondered if the one with tires worked.

No other buildings were in view, but the narrow road took so many twists that no structure would be visible even if there were any nearby.

Still, she had to assume this shack was isolated. This was not necessarily a bad thing. It meant the only people around were the ones she'd seen. With Desano gone, that left three men and a woman for her to deal with.

As she watched, the man they had called Leonardo approached the shack. Brooke scurried back to her cot, lay down, and closed her eyes.

"I have brought you something to eat and some water."

Brooke stirred as if just awakening and opened her eyes. She sat and took the plate he handed her. "Thank you."

"Tonight, if Estaban is lucky, we will have rabbit to go with our rice. If he is not..." He shrugged. "We eat beans and rice again. In this country we are used to eating like this." He eyed her. "You are used to finer food."

"I am blessed, yes." She met his gaze directly. "But I know what it is like to have only simple food."

"Do not try to make friends with me with your lies," he snapped. "I know that all *Americanos* eat their fill of rich food every day while we go hungry."

"I know there are many hungry in your country." Brooke thought of the girl she captured. "But we have hungry people in my country too. That side is not shown to the world, but it is there."

"I do not think there are any as hungry as most who live here." He shoved a cup of water at her and walked away.

Brooke stared at his back. Did he feel it was a competition?

As she ate, she thought about the situation. He referred to their location as 'here,' as in this country. They'd brought her across the border. How did they do it? More importantly, how far were they into Mexico? Just across the border or deeper? How long had she been unconscious? Had it been hours or days? She ignored the dull ache in response when she shook her head. *Surely not days.*

The longer she was out, the farther they could have brought her, and the more difficult it would be for her to return home once she escaped. She put a spoonful of unflavored rice into her mouth and chewed slowly. As she ate, she considered what she did know about the situation.

They were getting water from somewhere. The water they first gave her was poured from a bottle, but it wasn't bought. It didn't taste like processed water. The water he just provided her was in a cup. It could've come from a bottle, but they wouldn't have carried enough water for five people. Six, counting herself. Besides, they were used to the local water, so it wouldn't matter to them. She closed her eyes.

Please, Lord, don't let me get sick. It's going to be hard enough getting away if I'm at full strength. I'm sure I don't have time enough to recover from anything.

She flexed her arm. It was sore but it didn't hurt as much as it had at first. That had to mean it wasn't infected. She thanked God for that and that it was her arm that was wounded and not her leg. Her legs would need to be at full strength. She forced her thoughts back to their source of water.

There had to be a stream. Eventually a stream flows to larger bodies of water. To the Rio? Or to the gulf? How far before it reached wherever it was going? What was the land like on the way? Scattered villages huddled along the banks, most likely. Water was too scarce not to take advantage of it.

She put down the empty plate and cup and lay down with her eyes closed. After she got away, she'd worry about all that.

Five days. That's what she had. Maybe not that if Desano got tired of waiting and came back sooner. And what if their friends came before that? How many others? Would it just be those carrying drugs or did they plan to have a meeting with... She frowned.

153

How many others? What about the partners they mentioned? They sounded frightened of them. There was always somebody more powerful to contend with.

She had to work on that window. It was her only chance out of here. Even when she was in top condition, she couldn't handle four people. Especially not armed. No, it had to be the window.

When they took her outside to relieve herself, Brooke heard the soft sound of water flowing off to the right. It wasn't loud enough to be a large stream, but it had to be the source. Out here she could see that the slight downward slope of the land was in the direction of the sound, even though hills were all around.

A few tuffs of green grew along the narrow footpath going down the slope, and this was an area where the trees managed to survive.

"Is that where you get water?" Brooke pointed toward the sound as she asked the woman.

Sonia hesitated. Then she shrugged and answered. "Yes. We do not have fancy water from the *supermercado* as you have in your country. We have to use what water we can find." She glared at Brooke. "You are not used to it. Perhaps you will get sick."

"I hope not." Brooke took a deep breath. *May as well give it a try.* "Who is this Manuel I heard you talk about?"

Sonia lifted her chin. "Manuel is *mi esposo*, my husband."

"Where is he?"

"Wherever you gringos put him."

"He was captured after he crossed the border?"

"It is not that simple." She frowned. "Manuel, he was going to see to our business in Houston." She hesitated, then shrugged again. "There was a battle and you gringos caught him." Sonia's stare on Brooke hardened. "We will give you to them, and they will

154

send Manuel home to me." She motioned with her gun. "Enough questions. You will go back inside."

She must be talking about the shoot-out, Brooke thought as she followed Sonia's orders. *I have even more of an incentive to get away. They told us at the academy exchanging hostages is against policy even if no one is killed. In this case, we lost an agent. Manuel will be lucky if he doesn't get the death penalty.* Brooke frowned. *I hope it takes Desano the full five days to realize that there will be no exchange. I need enough time to get that window open and get out of here.* She closed her eyes, took a deep breath, and released it slowly. Then she prayed. *With Your help, Lord. With Your help I can do all things.*

CHAPTER TWENTY

"THAT'S IT, FOLKS. Let's call it a day," the officer in charge announced. Darien stood and clamped his teeth together. It was getting too dark to see, and he knew it. But he didn't have to like it. Although every person on every one of the properties in the area had been questioned, the patrol still didn't have a clue. To continue looking in this area was illogical. Still, his anger was strong and nailed in place as he walked back to the car. Jack walked silently beside him.

"I'm sorry we couldn't find her," Jack said as they got into the car.

"Yeah. I am too." Darien started the car and drove onto the road. "Sorry I kept you so long after we should have clocked out. I should've told you to catch a ride back with another team. I hope I didn't mess up your plans."

"It's okay. I understand. I didn't have anything important to do." He glanced at Darien. "Besides, I couldn't leave. Partners stay together, right?"

"Yeah. Right."

Brooke wasn't with her partner. He didn't want her to be wounded, but a minor wound would be okay if it meant she was safe and would soon be back with him. He just wanted her home.

It was difficult, but he forced himself to stay within the speed limit. No need to go fast. It wouldn't help Brooke and might get somebody else hurt. His mind churned as he made his way to town.

What had happened and why? What did Brooke and Alonzo come across that led to this? It had to have something to do with the car they stopped. That was the last thing she mentioned when she called in. But what? If he knew, maybe it would help him decide what to do next. He frowned. Alonzo couldn't explain what happened. There was a chance he'd never be able to.

Darien stopped at a red light a few miles from town. *I don't know what Alonzo did, but I know this is his fault. He did something stupid. Brooke never would.*

Darien went over the scenario in his mind. Brooke mentioned an emergency stop concerning a car. She gave their location and reported her partner had gone to help civilians. When they tried to reach her later, she didn't answer. After that, nothing.

If the patrol wasn't shorthanded, agents would've responded faster. If not for those bombs, they would have more personnel and they might've been able to prevent whatever took place. If none of this had happened, he'd be with Brooke right now instead of driving back to town without any idea where she was.

He screeched to a stop for a red light he almost missed. While he waited for it to change, he took many deep breaths and released them slowly. He wouldn't help Brooke if he hit a pedestrian or another car.

The light changed and he drove to headquarters with his mind on what he was doing.

They assumed she was all right. They hadn't found anything to tell them differently. Darien had to cling to the hope that she was okay. Otherwise… If the blood at the scene was hers, it wasn't enough to indicate her life was in danger. He took another deep breath as his heart tried to race.

But where was she? Was she hurt worse that the blood indicated? Many injuries didn't involve blood, but they were serious, even life-threatening. Again he forced himself to calm down, but his mind stayed on the situation. Was that why she hadn't contacted anybody? His stomach clinched at the possibility. Did somebody take her? What were they into that they took a chance and kidnapped a federal agent?

He considered the information given at the latest briefings. A reliable source reported terrorists had joined with drug smugglers. He didn't want to think of what it would mean if Brooke was in the hands of terrorists.

No agent had been kidnapped before and the drug trade had been a problem for years. The only difference he could think of now was the terrorist angle. He shook his head as he recalled what'd been done to hostages in other countries. For the first time in a long time, he found himself praying. *Please let there be another explanation. Please let us find her all right.*

By the time Darien reached headquarters, he had come to a decision.

As soon as he and Jack clocked out, Darien went to Commander Young's office.

"Commander, someone must have abducted Brooke. The man found dead at the scene was most likely a Mexican. What if his gang took her across the border? There isn't any other explanation. We have to go get her."

"Have a seat, Agent McKee."

158

Darien continued talking as he sat on the edge of the chair. "We have to do something,"

"Our people have come to the same conclusion. We're investigating the situation."

"Then what's the next step?"

"We're talking with the Mexican Government as we speak."

"What's there to discuss? Someone took her across the border. We've got to get her back. Simple as that."

"Nothing is as simple as that. We can't raid Mexico. We've done too much invading of late. We must have the cooperation of the Mexican Government if we stand a chance of getting Agent Hudson back."

"We don't have any idea how much time we have."

"Neither do we have any idea where they're holding her. We don't even know *who* is holding her or why. I know you're anxious to get her back. So are we. But it won't do any good to go if we have no idea where she is. We have to wait until someone makes contact. Then we'll have a clue about what's going on and can plan accordingly."

Darien hated the idea of just waiting. Neither did he appreciate the reality that they had no inkling where she was being held. He didn't like a single thing about the situation. "What are we going to do if the Mexican Government drags their feet on this?"

"What we're going to do is the only thing we can do—wait for contact from whoever is holding her."

"What if the Mexicans give us a hard time?"

"Their government has a problem with the drug trade too. We're sure that they'll cooperate." He stared at Darien. "Go home, Agent McKee. Get some rest. I'll notify you as soon as we hear something. You think you can patrol tomorrow?"

"Yes, sir." Darien sat a few seconds longer. Jack had better go easy tomorrow. None of this was his fault, but that wouldn't keep him from seeing Darien's frustration. "They'd better contact us soon, or I'll go look for her. I'll find her if I have to search the whole country."

"I'm not going to point out how illogical that is. Go get some sleep. You want to be rested so you can be in on it when we make a move, don't you?"

"Yes, sir."

"Then go home. We'll call you as soon as something develops." Darien stood, but didn't move away. "Agent McKee, we'll get her back."

"Yes, sir."

Darien left the office. The commander was right, but he didn't have to like it.

When he arrived home, he parked in Brooke's spot, but didn't get out of the car. Instead, he glanced at her apartment. *Where are you, Brooke?*

He stared a little while longer, then exited the car and went to his end of the complex. *Where do I start looking? How do I find her?*

When he entered his apartment, he noticed he had messages on his answering machine. It couldn't be anything important, but he played them back anyway.

"Darien. This is Leah. Please call me when you get this." Leah sounded as upset as he felt. He took the phone and went into the living room.

"What happened?" Leah asked as soon as she picked up. "Did they find her? I know you were at the scene. What happened to Brooke?" She didn't leave any space for answers, if he had any to give.

Darien filled her in on everything he knew. After he assured her he'd let her know as soon as he found out anything, he broke the connection. He held the dead phone for a long while, then he went to the kitchen.

He ate a meal he didn't want, choked it down without tasting, and tried not to think of what the dinner would be like if Brooke were with him.

The living room was dark, but he didn't turn on a lamp. Instead he sat on the couch staring at nothing, then went to bed at the appropriate time, but not because he thought he'd be able to sleep.

He slid into bed wondering how long he should stay put and what he'd do when he got up.

The next morning he reported for duty. As he drove, he searched the terrain for a clue. It wasn't logical since they weren't near Brooke's territory, but he looked anyway.

When the shift ended, he signed out, but he didn't leave the building with Jack. Instead, he went to see the commander. Maybe a miracle happened, and he received news that he hadn't had time to notify Darien about.

When he left the commander's office, Darien had no more information than when he'd gone in.

He drove up and down streets until dark, then went home. This time he only stared at Brooke's apartment a few minutes before he started across the lot.

"Agent McKee?" Darien, hand on his gun, turned quickly toward the voice. "Hey, wait a minute. Don't shoot. It's me. Paco."

"Paco?"

"*Si.*" The young man walked from the shadows at the side of the lot.

"Where did you go the day the bombs went off? Where have you been since? I have some questions for you."

"I gotta talk to you too." Paco glanced around. "Can we go inside your place?" Darien just stood glaring at him. "Look. I ain't got nothin' on me." Paco opened his jacket and took it off. "I ain't never had nothin'. Not even on that day." He held out his arms to the side and turned around slowly until he faced Darien again. "I have to talk to you about Agent Hudson."

"Brooke? What do you know about what happened?" Darien closed the space between them. Paco took a step back.

"Listen. I will tell you all I know, but please, can we go inside?" He looked around again. "I don't think it's safe talking out here."

"Come on in."

Darien led him up the steps. As soon as they were inside, he turned to Paco and stood almost toe to toe. "Talk. What did you have to do with her disappearance?"

"Nothin'." Paco held up both hands. "I swear I ain't had nothin' to do with that." Paco took a step back, glanced at the wall, then the floor. "That day, they told me they were gonna blow up the parking lot. I didn't want Agent Hudson to be walking past when it happened. That's why I kept talking to her. She always been good to me."

"Why the parking lot?"

"They said if they destroyed all the cars, agents couldn't patrol. That way more of my people could come over."

"Your people? I thought you were born here."

"Just 'cause I was born here don't mean I ain't got people across the border." He gestured toward the south. "These men I know, they didn't say nothin' about blowing up no building. Lots of people were always inside that place. Many I knew when I saw them." Paco shook his head. "I wouldn'ta kept quiet if I knew."

"What does this have to do with Brooke?"

"Nothin'." He shrugged. "At least not what I hear on the street. Somebody else done it."

"What did you hear?"

"I hear they want Manuel back. You got him in—"

"Manuel? Who's Manuel? Who wants him? What does somebody named Manuel have to do with Brooke? Where is she?" Darien grabbed the front of Paco's shirt.

Paco released a hard breath. "Agent McKee. Please. I...I am trying to tell you. You...You got to let me tell you."

Darien released him. "Talk."

Paco stared at him for a few seconds, then started pacing. "See, you got two groups." He held up two fingers. "You got one group dealing drugs." He bent a finger. "And the other..." He folded the other finger down and frowned. "I ain't sure exactly what they into, but they hooked up with the drug people."

"You're pushing drugs."

"No way." Paco held up his hands. "I ain't never touched that stuff. I seen what it can do." He looked at Darien. "But I hear the drug people, they use the money to take care of a lot of their people in many villages."

"They get the money from my people who use the junk and destroy their lives."

"I know. I know. I tell you I seen what it does to some of my friends. I swear, I ain't havin' nothin' to do with drugs. I'm just saying..." He frowned. "Anyway, them others, not the ones with the drugs, but the others, they the ones who blow up the building. They the ones who tell me they gonna help fix things by messing up patrol cars so my people can come here." He held out both hands. "They don't say nothin' about blowing up the building. Nothin'." Paco shook his head. "They scary, but..." He shrugged. "If more people get through it's what I want too, so I join up with them." He

163

frowned and started pacing. "I seen them once right after the building blew up. I ain't seen them since. I went by their place later, and they're gone. They ain't left nothin' behind." He swallowed hard. "It looked like they ain't never ever been there." He blinked hard. "The headquarters building that day, it was terrible. I hope I never see nothin' like that again."

"What does that have to do with Brooke?"

"Nothin'. They ain't the ones who took her."

"Then who did? Talk."

"This drug group, that Manuel, he's their leader. You got him. He was the one caught."

"A few days ago?"

"Yeah. I heard on the street that his people took Agent Hudson 'cause they want to trade her for Manuel." He stopped walking and stared at Darien. "The government ain't gonna make the trade, are they?" His voice got lower. "They ain't gonna never give them Manuel and get Agent Hudson back, are they?"

"The government doesn't trade."

Paco nodded. "That's what I heard." He touched Darien's sleeve. "Agent McKee, you got to get her back before they give up trying and do something bad to her."

"I'd already be gone if I knew where to look."

"I got an idea of where they might be."

"How do you know? Where?"

"I know someone who's been to their place in Monterrey. I think I can find them."

"Monterrey's a big place. You got to give me more than that."

"I'm not sure how to tell you." Paco's gaze was steady. "I got to show you."

"You want us to go together?"

164

"That's the only way I know to help. Somebody I grow up with deals with them. When I hear about Agent Hudson I ask questions from him. I think I can find it from what he told me, but I don't know enough to tell you how to get there. I got to see it."

Darien stared at him for a long while. Then he shook his head. "I don't like it, but you're my only lead. Let's go." Darien started for the door.

"Hey, wait." Paco touched Darien's sleeve again. "We can't go now. We got to get some sleep and leave in daylight."

"I don't want to waste time."

"Officer McKee. We can't do nothin' this late at night. We can't even find a way to travel after we cross the border. We got to have wheels from over there, and we can't take your car where we're going. You got that patrol sticker telling who you are. You gonna walk two hundred miles? Even if we could, it would take too long. We sleep and go in the morning. Then you buy a car across the border and we'll be good to go. We get there faster that way. Okay?" Paco sounded as if he was talking to a child.

Darien hesitated. "Okay," he finally said. "But we leave at first light." He stared at Paco. "And you stay here."

"I ain't going nowhere. Not after I been here. I don't know who seen me. They might come after me. I don't think they like that I didn't go back the day after the bomb. That might be why they had moved when I went a few days later."

"You're probably right."

"Okay." Paco nodded and grinned. "I don't guess you got nothin' to eat, huh?"

Darien stared at him, then took Paco to the kitchen. "I got eggs."

"That's cool. I like eggs. Hey. You want me to cook them? My *mamacita*, she teaches me to cook. She say even though I'm a *muchacho*, I need to know how to feed myself."

"I'll cook. You sit."

As he fixed the food, Darien couldn't help think of how he and Brooke ate their meals together. He had to find her. They hadn't had nearly enough time together. He shook his head. A lifetime wouldn't be long enough. He had to find her before... He beat his anger out on the eggs.

I have to find her.

CHAPTER TWENTY-ONE

BROOKE WORKED ON the window for two days. Her captors left her alone for the most part, and she used the time well.

She started each day with a prayer. Before she even opened her eyes, she gave thanks for her deliverance. Every chance she got, she dug the handle of the fork into the crevice she'd widened all around the window, but she spent most of her time working on the bottom. Every minute she could she dug, ignoring the pain it caused in her arm. She prayed steadily as she worked. Her head still ached whenever she made a sudden move, but she kept at it anyway. Better a little pain and to be alive than be dead and feel nothing. She was convinced they intended to kill her.

This morning breakfast was over, and she was alone. She glanced at the door, then satisfied nobody was near, she gave the window frame a hard crack with the palm of her hand. After another look at the door, she put all her weight against the window frame and pushed. The window budged. The movement was too slight to measure, but that didn't keep her from hoping. She dug faster and harder.

When they brought her noon meal, she didn't eat it right away. Instead she drained the water from the cup, then held it out and asked for more.

"You are not feeling so good?" Sonia asked as she filled it again. "You have a fever? Perhaps you are getting sick from your arm. Perhaps you will need *un* médico when you go back to your people." She held up her own arm. "My arm, it is fine where you shot me." She glared at the empty cup. "I am used to the things in my country that make *gringos* sick."

"I'm just thirsty," Brooke said. "It's dusty in here, and the air is very dry."

"I am sorry we do not give you the fancy house your kind is used to, but we stay in this same place with you, and we do not complain." She poured water into the cup.

"I was not criticizing. I'm just explaining why I'm so thirsty." Brooke drained the cup and held it out again. She worked hard not to show that it was a struggle to fit more water into her already full stomach.

Sonia stared at the cup, then at Brooke. "I will not stay here and tend to you. I am not your maid." She shoved the bottle at her, glared, then left the shack.

Brooke put the bottle to her lips, but she didn't drink. Instead she put the top on the bottle, set it on the floor beside her cot, and smiled. Good. She'd need something to carry water in after she got out.

She finished eating and went back to work on the window. After about two more hours, her arm protested strongly, but the window creaked open a little.

Brooke breathed in the fresh air deeply, then forced herself to pull the window closed. After the evening meal she worked on the window more. Finally she was able to shove it open wide. Soon, she promised herself as she pulled it closed.

She rubbed her arm and lay down. It was still early evening, but she made herself rest. She would need all her strength to get away. This was her last night as their hostage.

Brooke didn't know what time it was when the sound of a car woke her, but it was still dark. The faint noise grew louder by the minute.

"Manuel," Sonia shouted as she and Estaban rushed from their cots and left the shack.

As soon as they were out the door, Brooke stood on the cot and shoved the window open. This was it.

She tucked the water bottle into her back pocket and hoisted herself up. Ignoring the protest from her healing arm, she scrambled out the window and dropped to the ground outside.

A new loud, cold voice at the front of the shack called for Desano.

Brooke frowned. Without glancing back, she ran as fast as she could down the hill leading to the stream, praying she wouldn't trip over something in the weak light the sliver of moon provided.

Before she could reach the creek, gunfire forced her to find cover. She sprawled behind a tree at the side of the path and looked around for something, anything, to use as a weapon. More shots sounded and this time several yelps of pain mixed in.

Brooke grabbed a short, thick stick and pulled. *This will have to do for now,* she thought. She gripped one end, held it tightly, then lay staring at the back of the shack. *Lord, please keep your hedge of protection around me.*

No one came into sight. Brooke realized the shooting wasn't at her. It was coming from the front, and it sounded as if a lot people were trying to empty all the ammunition they had.

Heavy as it was, the gunfire stopped almost as soon as it started. Brooke stayed in place. Someone in the shack shouted to someone outside in a language that wasn't Spanish or English. She tried harder to blend in with the brush.

A car door slammed, and she assumed it was to the same vehicle as before the shooting. It drove away. The sound of the motor faded, but Brooke stayed where she was.

Finally, when there was no other sound except that of night animals, she rose to her feet. Still grasping the stick tightly and praying, she slowly, quietly, crept up the hill to the back of the shack. She stood with her back pressed against the adobe wall and listened. No human sounds reached her.

She took a deep breath, crouched as low as she could, then peeped around the side.

Heavy smoke drifted from the front and off to the side as if trying to sneak away from what happened. A night bird flapped away.

Brooke, sliding slowly along the side wall, made her way to the front of the building and stopped.

The smoke was thicker, but not so much that she couldn't see bodies scattered in the clearing like debris tossed by a storm.

Brooke paused and gave thanks to the Lord she fled the shack in time. That she wasn't caught up in the carnage.

Quietly but quickly, Brooke approached the first body. Estaban's hand was stretched out as if reaching for the gun a few inches from him. Brooke picked it up and checked to make sure there was still ammo. He appeared dead, but Brooke checked for a pulse to make sure. Nothing. Then she checked the others. They were beyond help too. She stood and looked around.

The ones she knew were joined in death by two men Brooke hadn't seen before. These must be the partners she heard them talking about. They were not Mexicans. If she had to guess, she'd say they were Middle Easterners. She looked around a few seconds longer, then went to work.

She searched the bodies. She found money, a few of scraps of paper not written in English, a small key in the pockets of one of the strangers, and a knife on Estaban. She tucked everything into her own pockets and moved on.

Leonardo had a cell phone as did the other stranger. Brooke tried both, but couldn't get a signal. She tucked them away too. None of the dead had identification.

Brooke frowned. She recalled bits of conversations she overheard about the group Manuel tied them to. Maybe something she heard or found would be helpful if she could reach headquarters. She shook her head. No. The good Lord willing, it was not *if*, but *when* she got to headquarters.

A search of the cabin turned up nothing useful but empty water bottles. She didn't dare take time now to go to the creek, but maybe they'd come in handy later. She hurried back outside with two of them.

She had to get out of her uniform. She'd probably come in contact with people on the way home and not everybody liked her government.

After she tugged the jeans off Sonia and put them on, she looked at the shirts on the bodies. Blood soaked.

Her things and the things from the others went into her pockets. She rolled her uniform pants as tightly as she could and pushed them under a bush to the side of the driveway, then brushed dirt over them. That might buy a little more time. Next she took off her uniform shirt.

Using the knife she obtained from Estaban, she cut off her other sleeve and tore the insignias from the pockets and shoulders and hid them all in a clump of scrub grass further away.

She pulled the shirt back on and unbuttoned the top three buttons and pressed the flaps back. Then she tucked the collar inside. At least someone would have to get close to realize the shirt was part of a uniform. She worked fast. How long before Desano returned?

Sending up another prayer, she gathered the guns and hurried to the car that still had wheels.

She lost a little of her tension when she saw the key in the ignition. A little more fled when she saw a bundle of T-shirts on the back floor. Maybe that was what Sonia used as 'her baby.' Brooke shed her own shirt, and pulled on a wrinkled tee.

One handgun she tucked into the back of her waist and pulled the shirt over it. Then she threw some of the guns in the trunk, but kept two others with her. She grabbed the cap from the back seat and tucked her hair under it.

She slid into the car, set one handgun beside her, and shoved the other under her seat. Ignoring the heavy dust cloud she created as she turned the car around, she drove down the rutted driveway as fast as she dared.

Once she reached the end, she glanced down the road in each direction. She was glad the road was empty. That meant that the gunfire hadn't attracted attention.

She closed her eyes, prayed, then turned left toward the hills. She knew from the sun's path when she was in the shack this direction was north. Now the dipper showed her the way.

If she could reach higher ground, maybe she could see lights from a village, a house, a fence, anything to give her some idea of which way, which roads, would take her closer to home.

As she drove in the dark, she was thankful for the cover of night. She hoped she wouldn't meet Desano along the way, but if she did, the darkness might buy her a little time before he recognized the car.

If she was fortunate, the next people she would see would be friendly and would either give her directions to the nearest village or to the local police. Whatever happened, she was free now and one step closer to home. One step closer to seeing Darien again.

CHAPTER TWENTY-TWO

DARIEN SHOOK PACO'S shoulder. "Hey, wake up."

"Man," Paco said as he rolled onto his back. "What time is it?" He sat up, frowned, and stretched. "It's still dark outside." He squinted at Darien standing over him. "Man, you already dressed."

"By the time we get across the border, it'll be full light. We could have left half an hour ago. Get up and get ready. I have to make a call."

Darien didn't look to see if Paco followed orders. Neither did he hesitate as he called the commander at home. If waking Commander Young before daybreak was the worst thing against Darien after this, he would consider it a plus. If this cost him his career, so be it. Anything would be okay if it got Brooke back safely.

"I've got a lead I want to follow." He ignored the sleepiness in the commander's voice as he told about Paco and the information from him. Then, pacing the living room, Darien explained his plans. "Sir, we're crossing the border. I'm going to let Paco try to take me to the place the group works from. We leave as soon as I get off the phone."

"I was going to call you at a decent hour, Officer McKee," the commander said. "I guess this is it."

"You know where she is?" Darien stopped pacing. His grip tightened on the phone.

"No, but we did receive a demand for the release of this Manuel you mentioned. We questioned him. It didn't take long for him to give us information." There was no humor in the short laugh Commander Young released. "Manuel doesn't care to go back even if we're willing to trade. He wants to cut a deal. The group his gang has connected with would kill him because he got caught." Commander Young released another harsh laugh. "Manuel proceeded to tell us everything he knows about that group and their network. And he knows a lot. They have cells all over the country, but are concentrated in D.C. That's when we called in Homeland Security."

"Did he say where they might be holding Brooke?"

"Like your friend, Paco, said, it's not the drug group holding her. It's Manuel's gang. That's probably a plus."

"Did he give you specifics?"

The Commander hesitated. "We're waiting to hear from the Mexican authorities before we take any action."

"That might be too late."

"I know. I know." He told Darien what Manuel said about two possible locations. Then he paused. "You realize I'm not authorized to give you permission to go after her."

"I know, sir. I'm requesting personal leave," Darien said quickly.

"You've got it," the commander answered just as quickly. "Agent McKee, bring her back." His words were slow and hard. He hesitated a few seconds before he continued quietly. "You know we're shorthanded. Be careful. We need all the agents we have."

"I will, sir." Darien broke the connection, hung up, then turned to Paco. "I have an idea where to go to find Agent Hudson. I don't need you."

"Monterrey, right?" When Darien didn't comment, Paco continued. "Two will be better than one. I have cousins in that area. They could help us." Darien remained quiet. "Agent McKee, I owe it to Agent Hudson. You got to let me help get her back. Please."

"This will be dangerous."

"I know this."

"You could get hurt or worse."

Paco stared at Darien. "This I also know. I must help my friend."

After a few seconds Darien spoke. "Okay. Let's go."

In record time, but too many minutes later, Darien drove to the International Bridge and parked on the street. They walked across the bridge into Mexico.

Refusing offers of taxi rides, they walked the few blocks to a used car lot Paco told him about.

Once on the sidewalk in front of the lot, Darien stood and examined the selection of vehicles. Then he walked over to a mostly black Ford that was about ten years old.

"Do not be fooled by the outside, *mi amigo*," the salesman said as he came over. "Ugly cars are safer on the streets here as they are in your country. They run good. You will have no trouble. Where you going?"

"Monterrey."

"It will get you there with no problem. And back too, *mi amigo*," he added and laughed. "The motor is almost as good as when the car was new. It is a good car. The best I have. It will give you no trouble."

Darien had a feeling that the salesman would have said the same thing no matter which car he chose. He bargained because it was expected, but he would have paid more than the posted price if necessary.

As Darien drove away, the salesman was still assuring him about the condition of the car. Darien hoped the words were true enough to get him where he needed to go as quickly as possible.

Darien was in a hurry, but he couldn't shorten the distance.

A few hours later, they reached the outskirts of the city. Darien drove slowly around the perimeter, and Paco examined each side street carefully. Monterrey was a big place. They reached the far side when Paco yelled.

"Stop. Over there." He pointed to a side street. "There's the gas station. I remember because it's across the street from the store."

"We passed a lot of gas stations and a lot of stores. Maybe we should continue around and make sure."

"No, Agent McKee. The one I heard talking mentioned that his cousin owns the store named Garcia's."

Darien stared at the narrow storefront. "Do you know how many stores there must be in this city alone named Garcia's? It's a common name."

"I know this. I tell you, this is the way. Down this street."

Darien scrutinized Paco. Then he looked at the road. "May as well follow it. It's the only lead we have."

He turned down the road as it left the city behind. He glanced back once and hoped Paco was right. He had a feeling they couldn't afford to waste time on a futile chase.

Soon, the only buildings were scattered and parallel to the road, but a long way from it.

As Darien covered the miles taking them away from the city, the shacks became smaller and farther apart. He would have thought the places abandoned, but often he saw children playing in the dirt in front of them or someone sitting on a porch. Here and there he drove past spindly plants that looked as if somebody was trying to grow a garden. It seemed as if rain was needed here, just as it was in Texas.

Darien might've wondered if Paco had been wrong after all, or if maybe they had missed a turn, but there were no roads going off this one. Nothing except the narrow, rutted dirt driveways leading away. If he made a mistake, it was miles back to the city. Darien decided he had no choice except to go on. As they drove, he tried to ignore the possibility he was wasting valuable time—time that mattered to Brooke's safety. He pushed aside his second thoughts and kept going. For the second time in a long while, he prayed, and found it easier than the last effort he made.

The road seemed to wind and go on forever. They traveled miles without passing even a shack. The farther from the main road they traveled, the more Darien's mind filled with doubts.

Maybe Paco was wrong after all. Paco was certain this was the right way to go, but that didn't make him right. What if the house they were looking for was on a different road branching off the highway in Monterrey? Maybe Paco hadn't heard what he thought. After all, he was listening to somebody else's conversation. He wasn't part of it. Maybe Darien used up time he couldn't afford to waste.

He'd go a few miles more on this road, then he'd turn back and check in with the police. Could be that while he and Paco were on the way here, the authorities had obtained information that would lead to Brooke. A rescue operation might already be taking place.

Even as Darien had this last thought, he didn't believe it. He began to pray this time without thinking. He continued as he drove.

He turned a bend and continued to examine the land. He wasn't sure what he was looking for, but that didn't stop him from searching. Something on the right caught his attention. A narrow driveway led to the first shack they had seen for miles. Paco spotted it too.

"Agent McKee, look over there." He grabbed Darien's shoulder and pointed. "I think this is it," Paco yelled. "This is the road. It looks just like what the man said."

Darien turned onto the driveway without questioning Paco. Straddling the deep ruts and ignoring the dead brush scraping the sides of the car, he made his way toward the small building by following the several curves in what was supposed to be the driveway.

The scent of blood reached him before he was halfway there, before he could see the reason for the odor, but he had a good idea what caused it. He stopped the car so the driver's side was next to the brush and left the motor running. It was tight, but he managed to get his door open.

"Wait here, and stay inside the car," he whispered to Paco. "If you see me in trouble, get out of here. Slide behind the wheel as soon as I get out."

He drew his gun and eased onto the dusty path. In a crouch, he crept toward the shack.

The odor grew stronger. He stopped when he reached the source.

The remains of five bodies were scattered in front of the building. Vultures, disturbed by the human, flew away from their meal, but they didn't go far.

Darien released the breath he didn't realize he was holding when he saw Brooke wasn't one of them, but he didn't get his hopes up yet. He wasn't finished looking.

He went inside the shack, praying she wasn't in there either. It didn't take long for him to conclude the one-room shack was empty. He was thankful his prayer was answered.

Trying to ignore the smell, he checked the area around the clearing. He stopped walking when he came to a scrap of cloth under a bush. He picked it up and stared at it. A sleeve to a uniform. A Border Patrol agent's uniform. In the same area, he uncovered insignias from pockets and shoulders. Brooke. They could only be hers.

A search of the thick brush at the side uncovered Brooke's uniform pants under a thicket. Darien didn't care to guess what that might mean. He wanted to hurry, but was afraid of missing clues.

He searched the area around the shack in ever widening circles until he reached the creek. After he covered the surroundings several times and found nothing else, he went back to the car.

Miraculously, his cell phone picked up a signal. It was weak, but it was there. He notified the local police about what he found and the directions he took to get here, then walked back to the road.

Which way did they take her? Who had her now? He squatted and examined the dusty road. *God, I need Your help.*

He saw his own tracks, but although they were faint, he noticed other tire tracks going the opposite direction from which he and Paco came. He stared at them as if waiting for them to give orders or at least more information.

These could be old tracks, couldn't they? The car carrying Brooke could have headed the same way Darien came from. Just because he didn't pass a car didn't mean anything, did it? It could've left days ago. He had no time frame to work with. Was she

180

gone even before he left home? He prayed. "God, please help me find her."

A slight breeze blew as he examined the tracks. The cooling effect of the wind wasn't the reason his spirits lifted. As he looked, a thin layer of dust blew over the tracks, filling in part of them. They couldn't be very old, or they would have disappeared completely. Darien hurried back in the car. Thanks to God, he had a direction to follow.

CHAPTER TWENTY-THREE

BROOKE DROVE FOR so long she was no longer nervous about the narrow highway with no guardrails along the steep hill going down on her right. This road was better than the dirt one that had taken her away from the shack, and it was leading her farther away from the nightmare she'd been caught in.

She continued to hope for some sign of humans, but so far that hope hadn't been fulfilled. The greater prayer, however—the one that she wouldn't come in contact with anyone who would try to stop her—was still being fulfilled.

Night gave way to daylight. Brooke drained the last drop of water from the bottle hours ago and was thirsty again, but she forced herself to ignore the need as she continued to put miles between herself and the shack.

The hills were farther than they looked. Hours passed, but they still seemed as far as when she first saw them. She should have been exhausted from lack of sleep, but adrenaline kept her going.

After yet another curve, Brooke smiled for the first time since before she was taken hostage. She slowed and stared. There, in the distance, was a deep valley and buildings nestled in the hollow. A small patch of light hovered over them, more welcoming than the biggest neon sign in the world.

Smile still in place, Brooke followed the road winding between two more hills. The valley was now hidden by a hill, but that was all right. It was there.

The turns didn't bother her now. The road was definitely leading to a village. It was still a long way off, but she knew each mile took her closer.

Another car approached from the opposite direction, and Brooke moved a few inches closer to the cliff to give the car room to pass. She caught a glimpse of the driver as he sped past, and her heart jumped. Desano. Had he recognized her? She shook her head. It didn't matter who was driving—he had to have recognized the car. How long would it take to register?

She glanced into the rearview mirror just before the road twisted to the left again and saw his car stop suddenly. *Lord, help me.*

Brooke jammed her foot on the gas despite the sharp curve she drove into. Just before the turn took her out of sight, she caught a glimpse in the rearview mirror of the car following her. It rapidly closed the space between them.

After yet another sharp twist, she pulled the car into the narrow strip of dirt beside the pavement, grabbed the second gun from the seat beside her, and dashed toward the brush down the hill.

She fled at an angle at full speed. Desano would probably expect her to go straight down.

As she raced toward a small stand of scrub trees, she prayed she had enough time to reach it.

She ran until she heard the car engine just above her. Then she ducked behind a tree and waited. Only her gaze moved as she lay flattened between two thickets.

Desano stood at the top of the hill. Brooke could see his head move back and forth as he scanned the brush. When his searching stopped, and he seemed to be staring at her, she made sure her gun was ready. His gaze left her and continue to scan the thickets. Then, as she watched with her gun in hand, he started crashing straight down the hill.

Brooke heard him swear when he stumbled over something. His pace slowed as he stopped every few seconds, looked around, then moved forward. His movements took him away from her. Still moving at an angle and disturbing the brush as little as possible, Brooke crawled away.

Using whatever she could find for cover, she crawled up the slope and toward the road until she reached the top. Still on her stomach, she glanced at Desano.

He moved slowly, and he was still heading downhill and away from her. Brooke took a deep breath, then crawled onto the road and away from shelter.

Both cars were several yards behind her. Crawling military-style, she made her way back to them.

She prayed, took a deep breath, then rose just enough to see inside Desano's car. She debated whether or not to take his keys. The thrashing over the hill told her he wasn't giving up. He was still moving downhill, but he would hear if she turned off the motor he left running.

She jabbed the knife into the two tires on her side, then ran in a crouch to her car. A glance at the slope didn't reveal Desano.

Did he move farther down the hill or start back up? How long would it take him to return after he heard her take off?

Brooke slid behind the wheel, gunned the motor, and drove away as she slammed her door shut. As she pulled onto the road, she heard Desano yelling.

He reached the road and bullets bit into the ground to the side of her car. She pushed the gas pedal to the floor and swerved back and forth as if driving on ice.

She had to slow down for a curve, but raced around it as fast as she dared and followed the road to the village. Whenever she reached a straight section, she sped up. Soon, she would reach help.

The sound of a car behind her seized her attention. *No.* She knew who it was. Still, she glanced in her side mirror. The car behind her wobbled as it limped along.

A bullet hit the road a long way behind her, and she was thankful for the limited range of handguns.

Traveling on two flat tires, there was no way Desano could catch her before she reached the village. How long before the tires shredded away, and he drove on two rims? Was that possible? If so, would that slow him down even more?

As she drove she glanced in the rearview mirror from time to time. The distance between them was widening, but when she looked ahead, the village didn't appear much closer.

She chanted a prayer to stay calm. It didn't matter how quickly, she was going to reach help. There had to be some lawman in town, and most Mexican officials were as eager as the United States to stop the drug trade.

Another curve, and she couldn't see Desano's car anymore, but she could still hear him rumbling faintly in the distance. Then the sound disappeared. She was going to reach safety.

Ten minutes later, her car began to sputter and stutter. Then it rolled to a stop. The road sloped downward, but it wasn't steep enough to let her coast closer to the village. The gas tank was empty. When she reached the road, she should've taken Desano's car.

She shoved the second handgun into her waistband, grabbed the one from under her seat, got out, and ran along the road.

The sound of Desano's car was faint, but she heard it closing the space between them.

She ran as fast as she could for a short distance, then moved into the brush.

Uneven ground made the going rougher and slower, but she was safer and still moving toward the village.

As the sound of the car grew louder, Brooke moved farther down the hill and worked her way to where the growth was thicker.

Few trees grew on this hillside, and the nearest ones were either a long way ahead or a lot farther down the hill, but the brush just ahead of her was thick and high. Brooke hoped it was enough.

The car stopped above her and bullets ripped through the brush to her right. She had to find a good spot to make a stand.

Brooke heard small rocks tumble down the hill as Desano left the road. Now on foot, he crashed through the thick growth far behind her when his bullets clipped some bushes several feet behind her and to the side.

A heavier scrambling sound reached her, and many rocks skittered down the hill. She heard Desano cursing her and agents in general.

She was wearing Sonia's jeans and one of their T-shirts, but he must have recognized her.

Noises from him stopped, and she waited. Then they started again. He must have slipped coming down the hill. How much would that slow him? Brooke knew it was too much to hope he twisted something that would prevent him from closing in on her.

She scanned her surroundings, looking for a spot to make a stand. There was none. She thought about going back up to the road. Could she make it to his car?

When the shooting at her started again, and a bush near her lost half its growth, she made up her mind. She didn't stand a chance unless she faced him, and she'd have better odds if she did it up on the road.

Using whatever growth she could for cover, she moved in a crouch back up the hill as quickly as she could, praying she would make it.

CHAPTER TWENTY-FOUR

DARIEN DROVE THE narrow highway as fast as he dared. He knew his speed was unsafe, especially when he took the sharp curves, but that didn't slow him down.

The little voice inside him screamed for him to push the car to eat up miles as quickly as possible. It was usually right. He frowned. All these years. Was it the voice of God?

As Darien approached a sharp bend, noises made him roll down the window. He pulled over to the side as far as he could, brushed against the dirt on the hill, and turned off the motor. For a few seconds nothing interrupted the silence. Then the series of pops sounded again.

Darien looked around. "Gunfire. Where's it coming from?" he asked, though he knew Paco didn't have an answer.

The road in front of them was clear. He glanced in his rearview mirror. Nothing interrupted the view of the curves of the road behind them, either. He heard it again and knew it was ahead.

"Brooke," he whispered, and his gut clinched. It had to be her. The gunfire told him she was in trouble, but it also told him she was alive. He turned the motor back on and floored the accelerator. The car leaped forward as he pulled back onto the highway.

They rounded the next curve at top speed.

A figure appeared from over the hill and ran onto the road many yards in front of him, coming toward him. Maybe it was wishful thinking on his part or maybe it was something in the gait. Whatever the reason, he knew it was Brooke, and she was in trouble.

Darien demanded more speed from the car. It hesitated, then jumped to obey. The shimmy told him the vehicle had reached its speed limit, but he ignored the protest. He prayed it wouldn't shake apart before he reached Brooke.

Darien got closer and another figure approached from same the direction.

The first person was near enough for Darien to recognize Brooke. She faced her pursuer just as Darien's car reached her. Her eyes widened when she glanced his way, then looked back at her chaser.

Darien drove between her and the man. He put the car in neutral, opened the door without bothering to turn off the motor, and stepped out before the wheels even stopped turning. The vehicle chimed out a reminder that the door was open. Darien ignored it.

"Get on the floor and stay down," he yelled back to Paco.

Brooke closed the few feet between them and dashed behind the open door. She glanced at Darien and smiled.

"Darien," she whispered. When she looked at him like that, Darien knew all over again it would've been worth anything to see her face once more.

A shot from the man chasing her broke the front passenger-side window. Brooke answered with shots of her own.

A bullet slammed into the man's shoulder and he yowled as his gun fell from his hand. He looked at it, but didn't bother to try to pick it up. Instead, he placed his hand over his shoulder and raised the injured one.

Darien tried to convince himself it was a good thing the man was only wounded—maybe they'd obtain useful information from him. But a part of Darien regretted that this criminal who tried to kill Brooke still breathed.

"Face down on the ground," he and Brooke shouted at the same time. Brooke added "Desano" to her order.

The man wasted no time complying. Darien handed Brooke his handcuffs and smiled. As Brooke went forward, he kept his gun pointed at the man stretched on the ground, silently begging him to twitch just a little. Desano had better sense.

Brooke cuffed him. She and Darien dragged him to his feet, then over to Darien's car. There, they stood him up and pressed his chest against the side.

They searched him and found his wallet. In it were a few American dollars and some pesos, along with identification. Brooke removed a driver's license with a Brownsville address. It looked good, but Darien doubted if it or Desano's social security card beneath it were authentic. However, it was obviously good enough to get him across the border whenever he wanted.

"Agent Hudson, you are okay?" Paco scrambled from the back seat.

"Paco?"

"*Si*. It's me, Agent Hudson." He ran to her and wrapped her in a big hug. "I was so worried." He squeezed tighter. "You are all right. I am so glad."

"What are you doing here?" She glanced from Paco to Darien. "How did you two get together?" She turned to Paco and frowned. "And where have you been, Paco Suarez? I've been worried about you since that day you left us after the bomb went off."

"I will tell you everything. I promise."

"Paco can explain his story later," Darien said.

At the sound of sirens in the distance, all four looked in that direction.

"I called them from the house," Darien explained at Brooke's puzzled look.

"Good." She nodded. "I couldn't get a signal." She kept her gaze on him. "You were at the house?"

"Yes. That's where I found your uniform slacks, your sleeve, and these." He handed her the insignias he had picked up. "It's also how I knew which way to go from there."

"How did you know that?"

"I had help from God." He looked at her and explained about the tracks. "I could get used to this prayer thing," he said.

"It's not hard." She touched his hand and Paco's and gave a simple thank you prayer.

They didn't have to wait long for the police.

The officers approached Brooke and the others with their hands on their guns. Darien called to them and informed them he was the one who had called. With permission, he took out his identification. The police removed their hands from their guns and approached. One took out a pen and small notebook. Darien quickly explained the gist of the situation. Brooke stepped forward and introduced herself.

"*Si,*" the officer in charge said. He nodded. "Your government informed ours about you." He fixed Desano with a stare, and the prisoner stiffened. Then the officer looked back at Brooke and his expression softened. "It is good to see you alive."

"It's good to be alive." She smiled.

It didn't take long for Darien and Brooke to explain what had happened on the road and who Desano was.

"I know our government will be anxious to question him," Darien said.

The officer looked at them. "I am sure ours will as well. We have the same problems. I am just a policeman, but I believe our governments will work together on this matter. We are on the same page in this thing." He glanced at Paco. "It seems you already have a passenger for the back seat of your car, Agent McKee."

"Yes, Paco is a friend," Darien explained.

"*Bueno.*" The officer nodded. "If it is all right with you, we will take your prisoner to the police station. You can follow, but first we will search his car. You are welcome to watch."

Darien and Brooke observed the officer. A paper with Desano's demands for Manuel's release was balled up under the seat. They didn't find a cell phone, but they hadn't expected to. He probably used a throwaway and dumped it as soon as he made the demand for the trade. Darien wondered why he kept the paper. It wasn't needed and was just plain stupid. They didn't find anything else of importance.

The police put Desano into their car. "We will have the two cars towed, but I do not think it is necessary to wait for the truck." He looked at Desano. "This one will not have need of a car for a long time, if ever again." He turned back to Darien. "I will give you directions to the police station in case we are separated on the way back."

He gave the uncomplicated directions, then got behind the wheel of his car.

Darien pulled Brooke against him. "Baby, I thought I lost you. I was afraid they'd..." He held her at arm's length and studied her face. "Are you all right? We found your blood at the scene of the kidnapping." He touched her cheek, then her shoulder, and she winced. "They hurt you." He glanced at Desano in the back seat of the police car and shifted away from Brooke.

"I'm okay." She cupped her hand around his face and turned his gaze back to her. "A bullet grazed my arm, but it kept going. It's okay. Really."

"You're sure?" He glanced at the police car again, then back at her, and relaxed. It was all over. Brooke was safe and with him.

"Darien, I couldn't have run like I did if I wasn't." She shook his arm. "I'll tell you all about it later. For now, we'd better go. The officers are waiting."

"Go ahead and get in. I'll be back in a minute." Darien walked to the police car.

"Don't do anything dumb," Brooke called after him.

"I won't. I promise."

After a few minutes' conversation with the officer, he returned with a clipboard. He set it beside him and got behind the wheel.

"Start explaining," Brooke said to Paco as Darien started the car. "I want to hear all of it."

"I will gladly tell you everything I know," he said. "Those men, they did terrible stuff."

Darien followed the police car. As he did, Paco talked from the back seat.

He started with how he had met the terrorists outside the store one evening when he finished his shift. They walked with him and talked about how hard he worked.

"Those men knew I worked at the store, what hours I worked, and even what time I went to lunch. I worked a lot and it was not

fair that I should have to, they said. I thought they cared about me."
Paco paused. "My *mamacita* and you, Agent Hudson, were on my
back about me finishing school and how I should never have
dropped out. These men, they understood." He paused again. "I
went to a meeting with them and heard talk about how hard it was
for poor people. Those from Mexico should be allowed in to find a
better life, they said." Paco's voice lowered. "I went to one more
meeting and they told of their plan for the parking lot." Paco
pounded his thigh. "I did not like the sound of that, but I knew
there were many not as lucky as me. I did not help, but I didn't tell
on them either."

They listened as he explained everything.

Brooke and Darien exchanged looks. If that group was involved
with smuggling drugs as well as the bombing, they might still be in
the Brownsville area.

CHAPTER TWENTY-FIVE

BROOKE AND DARIEN watched as the officers exited their vehicles and removed Desano from the back seat.

Darien shut off the motor and unfastened his seatbelt, but just sat there. The police waited outside the building for them, but he made no move to exit. After a minute or so he called from the window.

"We have unfinished business. We'll come inside in a moment. Okay?"

"*Si*," the officer in charge said and pushed Desano inside the building.

"Darien?" Brooke had a puzzled look. "Is something wrong?"

"No." His answer was low.

He faced Paco, stared at him a few seconds, then handed him the pen and clipboard.

"Wait here for us. Write everything starting with the bombing. Tell how you didn't know they were going to bomb the building."

"*Si.* That is true. I will write everything." Paco glanced at Brooke. "I don't write so good. My English, it is not..." He shrugged and looked back at Darien. "Agent Hudson, she knows about my English."

"That's not important right now," Darien said. "What is important is what you have to say. Okay? You understand?"

"*Si.* Okay, Officer McKee." Paco bobbed his head several times. "Okay."

"You really didn't know their plans for the buildings, did you?" Darien's words held an edge.

"Yes. No. I mean no, I didn't know they were going to blow up buildings." His head bobbed up and down. "I thought they meant to fix it so the patrol wouldn't be able to use their cars to catch the ones coming from Mexico. That's all they said they were going to do. I told you that at home and again here."

Darien stared at the police station, then back to Paco. "Yes, I remember."

"If I knew what they were going to do, I would have told," Paco said. "I would have gone into the headquarters building and made somebody listen. I would not have let that terrible thing happen. I did not think that even if they only blew up the parking lot, people may have been there. I did not think that. You must believe me."

"Write everything you remember no matter if you think it's unimportant. Maybe you can tell us something that will help us get that group. You might know something that's helpful that you aren't even aware of."

"I hope so. I hope what I have to say will help nail them before they do something terrible like that again." Paco tightened his grip on the pen, but he didn't write anything. Instead he stared at Darien and Brooke and shook his head. "How could they kill just like that?

They knew many people were in those places. Why did they do it? Do they hate us Americans so much? Why do they hate us?"

"We don't know the answers, Paco," Darien said. "The important thing is to apprehend them before they do any more damage."

Darien thought of the senseless loss of life that day. The property loss was great. The destruction to the city and to the area surrounding all of the explosions was extensive. But nothing compared with the deaths. Things could be replaced, rebuilt.

"Agent McKee, I promise that I will tell all I know about those men."

He pulled his attention back to Paco and what he was saying.

He started writing. His pen moved fast across the paper. He was still scribbling as Brooke and Darien left the car and walked toward the building.

As soon as they entered the building, the chief introduced himself then led them to his office at the back of the building. Desano wasn't in sight.

"We have secured your prisoner. My government is working out the details with yours for the transfer," he said after they were seated. "My superior talked to those higher up. Because he abducted Agent Hudson, they will make an exception and release Desano." He smiled. "It is a shame he will not get to experience some time in a Mexican prison. If your government ever decides to release him, I am sure we will be glad to have him stand trial for his crimes here."

"I'm sure of that," Brooke agreed.

As she spoke, there was a knock on the door. The chief gave permission, and the door opened. An officer entered carrying a tray loaded with food.

"I understand you were the guest of our prisoner and his friends for a while," the chief said to Brooke with a smile. "You are probably hungry." He nodded to the officer, who handed the tray to Brooke.

"*Gracias*. Thank you very much."

Her stomach growled in anticipation, and she looked at him sheepishly.

"I can provide something to eat for you as well, if you wish," he said to Darien.

"No, thank you. I'm okay."

"If you will excuse me, there is a matter that requires my attention. The officer outside the door will be happy to assist you if you need anything."

"Thank you," Brooke said again as he left. She said a blessing for the food, for her freedom and her thanks to all involved. She included a special prayer for Darien and Paco. After that, she began to eat.

Darien turned to Brooke. "Do you have any money on you?"

"I found a little on the bodies when I was searching for weapons. Why?"

"I have something in mind. May I have it? I'm going to put it to good use."

"Sure." She handed him what she'd taken from the bodies.

"I'm going out to talk to Paco," Darien said as he stood. "I'd tell you to enjoy the food, but I can see that you already are. I'll be back soon." He grinned then he kissed the top of her head and left the office.

"HOW ARE YOU coming along?" Darien asked Paco when he got back to the car.

"I have just finished." He handed the clipboard to Darien, opened and closed his hand, and stretched his fingers. Darien read it carefully.

Paco included how he was afraid to go to the police because he knew the men would kill him if they found out. When curiosity got the better of him, he went back, but the terrorist's hideout was deserted. When he heard about Brooke's kidnapping, he went to find Darien.

Darien looked up from the clipboard. "This is good. You can get out of the car." He hesitated and stared at him. "You have family nearby. Right?"

"*Si*." Paco nodded. "My *tia*, my aunt, and some cousins, they live not very far from here."

"Good." Darien held out the keys to the vehicle and the money he received from Brooke. Then he took out his wallet and removed all his cash. "Here."

Paco stared at Darien, then at what he was offering, but he didn't accept them. "Officer McKee? I don't understand."

I think you should visit your aunt and cousins for a while," Darien said. "You might get in trouble if you go back home right now."

"Our government, they would not believe me when I say I have nothin' to do with the bombings?"

"They don't know you as we do. You took a chance by coming to me, and you helped find Brooke."

Paco continued to stare at Darien. "You really think I will be in big trouble if I go back to the States now?"

"No sense taking a chance."

"My *mamacita*, she will be worried when I do not come home."

"Officer Hudson and I will go talk to her. I don't know how long you'll have to stay away. We'll let her know when you can come back, and she can tell you." He smiled at Paco and held out the keys and money again. "Consider the car a gift as well as the money."

A stunned Paco stared at him. "I...I don't know what to say. I...I... *gracias*. Thank you. I thank you for everything. I am glad we got Agent Hudson back."

"So am I, Paco. So am I."

Paco shook Darien's hand for a few seconds before he let go. After hesitating, he grabbed Darien in a quick hug. He grinned, let him go, and stepped back. "Give Officer Hudson a hug from me too. Okay?"

"Will do. You stay out of trouble, Paco."

"I will, Officer McKee. You can count on it. I will stay out of trouble. I have learned from this experience."

Paco was still thanking him as Darien walked back to the building to join Brooke.

CHAPTER TWENTY-SIX

"YOUR GOVERNMENT WILL share with us any information it obtains from interrogating him that might be useful to us." The police chief smiled as they stood. "We will now transport your prisoner to the bridge in one car." He looked at Brooke. "I personally will drive a second vehicle carrying the two of you. No further escort will be assigned." His jaw tightened. "It will be safer that way. He can provide valuable information to both governments, but we have decided that the fewer who know he is in our custody, the better for all." His stare hardened. "Not everyone will be pleased by his arrest." He stood a little straighter. "We are working on it, but we still have more to do to solve our problems with security."

"Thank you again for all you have done," Brooke said.

"I am sorry about the unfortunate circumstances you experienced here in my country. Perhaps you will visit us under more pleasant conditions?"

"I'm sure I will."

The three of them left the building together. Desano already waited in the first car. A second was parked for Brooke and Darien as planned. Neither was marked.

As they moved down the road, they simply looked like two vehicles that happened to be going toward the bridge leading to the United States border at the same time.

"With the information your government obtains, we hope to put a stop to this trafficking of poison that affects the people of both our countries. With the blessings of God, we will accomplish this," the chief said.

They rode the rest of the way in silence. Brooke felt herself relaxing the closer they drove to the border. Two and a half hours later, the bridge came into sight. Brooke looked at it in surprise.

"I had no idea they took me so far from the border. I didn't realize how long I was out." She turned to face Darien. "If Paco hadn't given you a lead, you never would have found me."

"Oh, I would have found you, baby. It would've taken me longer, and I don't know how I would have done it, but I would have found you."

"The Lord would've continued to guide you," Brooke said. She smiled.

"Yes." Darien nodded. "I can't dispute that. He had his hand in this situation more than once."

Brooke squeezed Darien's arm.

"We are here," the chief said as he approached the Mexican checkpoint. "I will explain the situation to our guards. After we are permitted to pass, we will proceed to the guards at your government's checkpoint. They will have two cars waiting, one for you and one for your prisoner." He smiled. "Don't forget—come back and visit us."

"Yes, sir. Thank you again for all you did," Darien said.

"Yes, thank you," Brooke said. They each shook the chief's hand.

As planned, two unmarked cars waited just beyond the United States guardhouse. Brooke and Darien watched as a guard placed Desano into the back of one vehicle. After that car left, Commander Young exited the other and held out his hand.

"Welcome home, Agent Hudson," he said as he shook Brooke's hand. "You will report to medical for clearance."

"Yes, sir." She felt it unnecessary, but knew she couldn't win an argument against procedure.

"As for you," he said as he turned to Darien, "it seems you should review proper procedures."

"Yes, sir."

Commander Young paused. "Good work." He paused again. "I guess your Paco decided not to come home."

"He's spending some time with relatives."

"I see." Commander Young stared at Darien. "Homeland Security won't be too happy about that."

"Yes, sir."

"I guess he got away from you in the confusion."

"You might say that, sir."

"Homeland will get over it. Do you need a ride?"

"My car is a couple of blocks from here. After the long ride, we need to stretch our legs."

"I'll see you back at headquarters for debriefing." He looked at Brooke again. "If medical approves, report to my office after you leave there. I'm sure you have information of value to us. Again, welcome home."

"Yes, sir. Thank you."

203

After the commander drove away, Brooke and Darien walked to his car. They'd only gone a few feet when Darien's hand found its way around her waist. He squeezed, then moved his hand to hers.

When they reached his car, he turned her to face him. Their lips met, and it took all of her willpower not to deepen the sweet kiss. Slowly they let the embrace end.

"Welcome home, darling," Darien whispered. Then he held her close for a while.

"It's good to be here," she whispered back.

They stood like that for a while. Only the fact that they would be even closer soon allowed her to move away from him and climb into his car.

They held hands all the way to headquarters.

CHAPTER TWENTY-SEVEN

COMMANDER YOUNG AND other top-ranking officers debriefed Darien. Then he went to wait for Brooke outside the medical department. He stood as she came into the hall.

"How did you make out?"

"They cleared me." She grinned. "Did they debrief you?"

"Yes. All finished."

They walked to Commander Young's office. Brooke left Darien to wait while she went in for her debriefing.

Commander Young welcomed her back. "Before we begin, let me give you some good news. Your partner is healing. It will be a while before he's back to normal, but he will recover completely."

"He survived?" Wonder filled Brooke's words. "Thank the Lord." A weight lifted from her. Alonzo had appeared dead, but God brought him through. More proof of His goodness.

"I assume Agent McKee is waiting outside for you?"

"Yes, sir."

"Ask him to come in. I have information to share with both of you."

She wondered why, but she did as the commander said.

Brooke exchanged a puzzled look with Darien when he entered the office. The commander waited until they were seated before he spoke.

"I have an update pertaining to your ordeal. Desano started talking as fast as he could after he was told that his friend, Manuel, is cooperating. He gave information about his operation and what he knows about his partners. Several government departments combined efforts to act on it. Terrorist cells in several locations around our country were shut down and many members are in custody. Our government and the government of Mexico cooperated, and Manuel's group was stopped on both sides of the border. The pipeline was followed to its source in countries farther south." He nodded. "It will take a while before either operation functions again. If the Lord is willing, that will never happen." He smiled at them. "Enjoy your time off."

Brooke smiled as she left the office with Darien. Sometimes the good guys won.

"Alonzo is going to be okay," she said when they reached the hall. "I know he made me mad many times, but I'm so glad he survived." She exhaled slowly. "Looks like I have a week of freedom before I have to report for duty. How about you?"

"I have a week too." Darien smiled as he took her hand. "Any ideas how to spend it?"

"Probably the same ones you have—being together and being thankful," Brooke said with a grin.

"Those are good ideas, but not exactly the same as mine." He turned her to him, smiled, and dropped to one knee in the middle of the busy reception area.

"Darien? What...?" Wide-eyed, Brooke stared down at his grin.

"Brooke, we've come so far together. When we met we were both hurting and considered giving up. With you, I've learned the healing power of love. You also helped me find my way back to God. Please say you'll marry me. Spend the rest of your life with me."

She stared for a few seconds as his words sank in, then she grinned and lowered to her knees facing him. "Yes. Yes." She laughed as she flung her arms around his neck and gave him a quick kiss.

Then she gazed into his eyes. "With you, I too learned how love can heal."

Applause and whistles claimed their attention for a few seconds, then their stares returned to each other.

"Way to go," someone yelled.

They stood and kissed. Darien held her hand.

"Not to rush you or anything, but I think we should apply for a license right now."

"I won't change my mind."

"I didn't think you would, but the waiting period in Texas is three days, and that would give us only four days for a honeymoon. We could go across to Mexico and get married right away, but I don't think either of us is ready to cross that line again just yet."

"You're right about that."

"So, it's get the license now, right?"

"Right," she said. She took his hand, closed her eyes, and bowed her head. Darien did the same. "Thank You, Lord, for bringing us out of the ordeal safely, and thank You for sparing Alonzo," she prayed. Then, still holding hands, they walked to his car as everybody applauded again.

Fifteen minutes later, license tucked into an official state envelope, they left the office.

"Three days of waiting," Brooke said as they walked to the car. "We have a lot to do."

Darien stopped walking. "What? We can find a Justice of the Peace to perform the ceremony."

"Justice of the Peace?" Brooke shook her head. "Let's go home. This lesson is going to take a while." She laughed, then kissed him and held him close.

They went inside her apartment and Brooke just stared. It looked so normal. After all she went through, her home was the same.

"Let's sit in the living room." She smiled as she led him to the couch. She faced him. "Okay. Here is one big difference between men and women. A woman's wedding is very important to her. Its importance ranks just below the man she's going to marry." She grinned. "True, we don't have much time, but this will not be a quickie wedding. We have to check with Reverend James to see when he's available. I don't mind a ceremony in his office, but no way can I let anybody else perform the ceremony. Then I have to make sure Leah can be my attendant, so she won't drop me as her best friend." She laughed at the look on his face. "Don't worry." She patted his hand. "It will work out. I'm convinced this is God's plan and nothing can interfere with what He has planned for His children. You do believe that, don't you?"

"Yes. Too much has happened to bring us to this point for it not to be the design of a Higher Power."

"Okay. Let me make some calls." They kissed, then Brooke picked up the phone.

She grinned after the call to Reverend James. Her smile widened after she talked to her sister, then Leah. "Told you it would work out. Bobbi will be here tomorrow. She and Leah can be my attendants." She winked. "Now, let's see what I have in the fridge. We'll pull together a celebratory meal for the newly engaged couple who will marry in three days."

They kissed and held each other close. Then they parted, but held hands the few steps to the kitchen. They were proof that, with God, all things work together for good.

AUTHOR BIO

Alice Greenhowe Wootson grew up in a suburb of Pittsburgh, Pennsylvania. She attended Cheyney University and earned a Bachelor of Science Degree in Elementary Education. After graduating, she married and remained in the Philadelphia area. She earned a Masters Degree in Education and Reading Specialist Certification and taught in the public schools.

Alice is the award-winning author of ten romance novels and an award-winning poet. She is a member of the Philadelphia Writers Conference and The Mad Poets Society. She has taught writing workshops for numerous groups.

Alice Wootson is an active member of Enon Tabernacle Baptist Church of Philadelphia.

She spends any spare time she can find reading, writing, traveling, and enjoying her three grandchildren. She lives in Philadelphia with her husband, Isaiah.

She can be reached by e-mail at: agwwriter@email.com.

Thank you for your Prism Book Group purchase!
Visit our website to enjoy free reads, great deals,
and entertaining, wholesome fiction!

http://www.prismbookgroup.com

www.ingramcontent.com/pod-product-compliance
Lightning Source LLC
Chambersburg PA
CBHW070925250626
47159CB00009B/3127